"I wouldn't have come if I'd known there would be all this…water."

Willa knew how absurd that sounded, but she was so shocked by her son's request for swimming lessons.

"I'm sorry," Bruce said. "I wasn't expecting him to ask me. Still, maybe this is—"

She wheeled on him. "Mr. Lawrence, are you aware of how my husband died?"

"I am," Bruce said. "And I realize swimming might present a challenge for your boys."

"A crossword puzzle presents a *challenge*." Willa narrowed her eyes. "I watched my husband be pulled out to sea. I saw him go under the waves. I never saw him come up. You'll excuse me if I can't quite call that a challenge."

"I get that it's an unsettling thought for you. But everyone should be able to swim for their own safety. I'd never force them to, but Joe has asked. What if this could be a very safe place to make peace with some of it?"

She felt her chin jut out in defiance. "I don't need to make peace with any of it."

Allie Pleiter, an award-winning author and RITA® Award finalist, writes both fiction and nonfiction. Her passion for knitting shows up in many of her books and all over her life. Entirely too fond of French macarons and lemon meringue pie, Allie spends her days writing books and avoiding housework. Allie grew up in Connecticut, holds a BS in speech from Northwestern University and lives near Chicago, Illinois.

Books by Allie Pleiter

Love Inspired

True North Springs

A Place to Heal
Restoring Their Family
The Nurse's Homecoming
For the Sake of Her Sons

Wander Canyon

Their Wander Canyon Wish
Winning Back Her Heart
His Christmas Wish
A Mother's Strength
Secrets of Their Past

Matrimony Valley

His Surprise Son
Snowbound with the Best Man
Wander Canyon Courtship

Visit the Author Profile page at LoveInspired.com for more titles.

For the Sake of Her Sons

Allie Pleiter

LOVE INSPIRED

INSPIRATIONAL ROMANCE

LOVE INSPIRED®
INSPIRATIONAL ROMANCE

ISBN-13: 978-1-335-59711-3

For the Sake of Her Sons

Copyright © 2023 by Alyse Stanko Pleiter

Recycling programs
for this product may
not exist in your area.

For questions and comments about the quality of this book, please contact us at CustomerService@Harlequin.com.

Love Inspired
22 Adelaide St. West, 41st Floor
Toronto, Ontario M5H 4E3, Canada
www.LoveInspired.com

Printed in U.S.A.

That Christ may dwell in your hearts by faith;
that ye, being rooted and grounded in love,
May be able to comprehend with all saints what
is the breadth, and length, and depth,
and height; And to know the love of Christ,
which passeth knowledge, that ye might be
filled with all the fulness of God.
—*Ephesians* 3:17–19

In thanksgiving to all the wonderful people who made Yorkfield Presbyterian Church our home for over thirty years.

Chapter One

People had told Bruce Lawrence that Willa Scottson was not the victim of the most cowardly thing he had ever done.

They were all wrong.

Bruce stared at the sheet of paper outlining Willa's circumstances—facts he'd known and new, worse facts he hadn't. He wiped his hands down his face as dread flashed through him. In the space of a few seconds, it had become the worst of all ideas to spend these next three weeks at Camp True North Springs.

He grabbed the file marked "Family Histories"— why, *why* hadn't he looked through it before now?— and sprinted toward Mason Avery's office. Part of him wanted to just make a break for his car, but that was no way to leave a friend like Mason. Even for this.

He found Mason on a ladder on the big house's wide porch, hanging a "Welcome" banner from the eaves.

"Mason, I can't be here."

Mason looked down. "Sure you can. I think it'll be great to get shots of the families arriving." The man started down the ladder as if there was no problem at all. "Everyone will be too busy to go swimming today, so you're totally free to take photos."

"It's not okay." Bruce cast a glance down the gravel lane toward the camp-entrance gate, relieved to catch no sight of the yellow school bus that would soon deposit this session's group of families. "I need to leave. Now."

"Hey, I know it's a bit rough to have that one family here. A Florida drowning victim cuts close to home." Mason's face took on the compassionate look Bruce had come to know from the man. Such a look had left for a long time after Mason's first wife, Melony, had died. Bruce was grateful the look had returned, and he truly wanted to help out the mission of Camp True North Springs, but that wouldn't happen now.

"That's not it. Well, not exactly."

"The mom's whole stance on photos doesn't help— I get it."

Bruce felt his gut tighten. Mason didn't get it. "Yeah, but—"

"It'll be good for you. That whole thing knocked you for a loop back then. A widow of a drowning victim—"

Bruce grabbed Mason's arm. "Not *a* widow, Mason. *The* widow." He wheeled around, fighting the urge to look at the sky and groan *You gotta be kidding me* at the absurd coincidence that had just landed on him. For a guy who made his life facing all kinds of daring feats, the cowardly urge to run nearly swallowed him whole. "Willa Scottson. Mason, it's *her*."

Time seemed to grind to a halt while Bruce watched Mason connect the dots. "Come on, it can't be. Can it?"

Bruce glared at him. "How many Willas do you

know?" The woman's unusual first name would be burned in the back of his brain forever. She had twin boys—boys who now had no father. He *could not* be here when she arrived, which might be any minute now.

He started toward his car. He could pick up his gear and help Mason figure out another solution later. "I gotta go."

Now it was Mason who grabbed his arm. "Whoa. Hang on. I know the stories are similar, but you're sure?" His friend thought for a moment. "You never did tell me you knew her name."

Bruce knew more than Willa Scottson's name—he knew the way her husband died, the exact date of his drowning. Rick Scottson's death had been hounding him for two years. The first photo assignment Bruce had ever refused had turned out to have dire consequences. "I'm sure. I knew it the minute I saw her name, but I read the file just to be sure. It's her. Mason, I can't be here."

Just as the words left his mouth, both men looked up at the unmistakable sound of the camp gate's metal fence squeaking open. Bruce, who'd jumped out of four airplanes, felt his stomach drop. He started backing toward the house door behind him. "I'll just stay out of sight. I'll leave the minute I can. It's not fair to her or those boys."

"Her? Here? Now? Bruce, this is too wild to be a coincidence. You've got to see that." His friend had that look—the look of a man who'd witnessed all the amazing stories Camp True North Springs had seen since its opening. Stories Bruce was supposed to be documenting to help other people see and support the camp's mission.

Bruce groaned in frustration. "Don't pass this off as a God thing. Not now."

"The new friends are here!" Mason's son, Charlie, came running around the side of the house, full of enthusiasm to meet the four families who would spend the next three weeks sharing his home. "C'mon, Dad, let's go meet 'em. Mr. Bruce, you come, too. Mom's on her way from the barn."

Bruce was just aware enough to catch the term Charlie had used. "'Mom'?"

A bittersweet glint passed over Mason's eyes. "Yeah. He asked yesterday if he could start calling Dana *Mom*. He asked me first if I thought Melony would mind. There may or may not have been a few tears involved." Mason tugged on Bruce's arm in a way that would put Charlie to shame. "Another one of my 'God things.'"

Bruce pulled his hand from Mason's grip. "This is a terrible coincidence that can only make a lot of people miserable. Don't tell Dana. Don't tell anyone."

"This is no accident. Even you can't ignore the odds." Mason leaned in as the bus rumbled down the drive. "Look, she has no idea who you are. She doesn't want any photos taken of her or her boys. You're in the perfect position to take time and make peace with this… And I'm here to tell you, you've *needed* to make peace with this. For a long time." He fixed Bruce with a dark stare. "So yes, I *do* think it's one of my 'God things.' *Your* God thing. So stay on the porch if you have to, or come be the daring guy they say you are and take some photos. Just don't leave."

Bruce felt his teeth grind together. "Some speech. Full of orders."

"Yeah, well, I'm getting pretty good at that stuff now. Dana says it's a gift. She'd also tell you to go use yours."

A trapped feeling tightened around Bruce's ribs. "This is a bad idea."

Mason stepped off the porch and began walking toward the bus as its folding door swung open. "Charlie says God doesn't have bad ideas."

Bruce disagreed. God *could not* be behind this. God wouldn't ask that of him or of Willa. Nothing good could come of him being anywhere near that woman and her sons.

It was the worst idea ever, no matter what anyone said.

Willa Scottson looked around the serene landscape bustling with arriving families. *I don't belong here.*

It hadn't been her choice to come. Rick had been gone for a little over two years, but she wasn't ready for what the camp claimed to offer. She was bone-tired of mourning, but that wasn't the same thing as being ready to move toward healing.

No one had to tell her she wasn't okay. She was stalled and numb and dragging herself through the motions of life. She'd even stopped going church—that had always been Rick's thing, anyway.

Only church hadn't stopped coming to her. First, it was visits and casseroles. Then came the invitations to services and events. When they'd gathered the funds for her and the boys to have a three-week stay at this camp and covered the family's travel expenses, all those

compassionate Christians pretty much had Willa backed
into a corner.

"Look how big he is, Mom. He's a huge frog. And
he spits!" She tried to let Jack's happy endorsement of
the odd little frog fountain pull her out of her cranky
funk. Her twins deserved better than how she'd been
slogging through life lately. She'd never admit this to
anyone—especially anyone back home—but the allure
of Camp True North Springs wasn't any healing it might
offer her—it was the chance to let someone else have a
crack at healing the boys.

*Look at you, outsourcing parenting. Admirable, isn't
it?* She could feel her frown deepen and told herself to
look down at her sons and smile. Smiles never came
naturally anymore. They were obligations—a mask she
applied but never felt. "I've never seen a frog so good
at spitting before." The sheer absurdity of her remark
struck her. Willa really hoped it got easier from here.

"He's so funny," Joe said with a giggle. "Look at his
eyes."

The frog had absurd, bulging eyes. "Funny," she said.

A boy several years older than her twins dashed up to
Joe and Jack. "Franco is an important guy around here.
Hi, I'm Charlie. You guys must be Joe and Jack, right?"

According to the brochure the church had provided
with the gift of her trip here, Charlie was the son of
Mason Avery, the man whose family's land had been
transformed into the camp. The boy looked happy and
well-adjusted. It was good to see that. Willa lay awake
too many nights, wondering if Joe and Jack would ever
get over losing their father. She wouldn't—she knew

that down to the bottom of her soul—but she wanted better for her children.

Willa tried to take comfort in the fact that all the children around her, each family assembling in the small clearing, knew the same jagged pain of a lost member. Even so, she still felt isolated. A lost cause of a soul. She had to do better but had no idea how. Would this place show her?

Charlie and the boys had jumped into an instant conversation about the merits of frogs when Charlie waved to a man with a camera, taking photos of other families. "Hey, Mr. Bruce, take our picture with Franco!"

Willa stiffened, and the adults traded alarmed glances. She'd been told there would be a photographer here. She'd responded, in the strongest-possible terms, that she would not allow photographs of herself or the boys. The threat of photos had almost made her cancel the entire trip altogether, were it not for the absolute promise of the camp owners that they would honor her requirement: no photographs.

The photographer clearly knew her demand, based on the uncomfortable look he gave to Charlie's request. The tall, fit man with a baseball cap over thick dark hair and a backpack slung over one shoulder didn't take a single step toward her. He looked down and slipped the camera behind his back.

Mason Avery stepped in between Willa and the man. "Actually, Charlie," he began, "Mrs. Scottson has asked—"

"Battery's run out, Charlie," the photographer said, still looking down. "Maybe later."

"Okay, maybe later," Charlie said. He seemed unaware of the awkward moment that had just taken place. Instead, he looked up at Willa. "Can I show them their room? You guys have bunk beds!"

"Sure," Willa replied. Anything to get past the current tension.

With that, Charlie, Joe and Jack took off. They dashed across the gravel in the direction of a large barn-like structure Willa guessed housed the guest rooms—and the much-anticipated bunk beds. Joe and Jack hadn't stopped talking about the sleeping arrangements from the moment Willa had made the mistake of mentioning them. Their six-year-old hearts were beyond thrilled at the prospect of sleeping in bunk beds.

Dana Avery, Mason's wife and the other camp co-director, stepped up. "I want you to know we'll honor your request of no pictures," she said in a reassuring tone. "Even though Bruce will be here for most of the session, there will be no photos taken of you or your boys. You have my word."

It sounded so extreme when the woman said it. It *was* extreme. But so was the moment when the storm surge had swept Rick out to sea. And the horrible footage that had shown up on television over and over until it finally faded from the nightly news. So no, there would be no photos of her and the boys taken by any journalist, anywhere, whether it sounded extreme or not.

"I'm sorry for your loss," said the photographer. He sounded like he actually meant it. Then again, those words had come out of every reporter's mouth just before they poked their sensationalist noses into her heartbreak and then asked her some form of *What does it feel like to have your husband drown in front of your eyes?*

"Thank you," she managed to say without any real sense of gratitude. She wasn't grateful. If she was being honest, she was annoyed that she'd managed to land at Camp True North Springs at the same time as a photographer. It seemed a cruel coincidence, ready to demolish the small shred of hope she held that this trip might actually do some good. Even as the man quickly walked away to take shots of other families, some part of Willa wanted to pile the boys back into the bus and tell the nice older gentleman to take them right back down the mountain.

It took her a moment to realize Dana was talking to her once more. "The boys' eyes are extraordinary," she was saying. "Lots of people notice my green eyes, but theirs? It's a striking color."

People frequently commented on the twins' eyes. They were like little imps, with those green eyes and mops of red hair that never stayed combed—people noticed them wherever they went. Rick had taken such joy in how people were drawn to the boys. Her husband had been a middle school principal, and all the students had known the twins from the moment they were born.

Willa was ashamed of how she wished the attention would stop. How she longed to render herself and Joe and Jack invisible until she felt ready to rejoin the world. But when would that be? Ever?

"They get them from their dad." She loved the boys' eyes. Hers were also a softer green, but their brilliant-green ones came from Rick. Every once in a while, Joe or Jack would look at her just so, and she could see her husband. It hurt in the most bittersweet of ways.

"That red hair and those freckles," Dana said. "We'll need to be careful in the sun. I bet they burn easily."

"They do better than most," Willa replied. "We used to spend a lot of time at the beach." *Used to.* Water had become her enemy. It's why the desert felt like a safe place to try and yank herself out of this black hole of grief. The boys ought to have their mother back—if only she knew how to find her.

"Is he going to be here taking pictures the whole session?" Willa wished her voice didn't sound so panicked at the thought. It would be exhausting to spend all her time here avoiding this Bruce and his camera.

"He will be here, but not taking photos the whole time. We're very blessed to have Bruce this session as both photographer and lifeguard." She pointed off to the large pond Willa hadn't noticed. How had she not noticed a pond in any of the materials?

"We've had a stretch of drought," Dana went on, "but now our pond is finally big enough to swim in again. Thanks to Bruce, we can offer swimming and swimming lessons. Do the boys know how? You said you spend a lot of time at the beach."

"That was before," Willa snapped back sharper than necessary.

Dana placed a hand on Willa's arm. "Of course. That was a thoughtless thing to ask. I hope you'll forgive me."

"They don't swim anymore." Willa made sure her reply sounded like the declaration it was. "And I don't intend for them to start back up here."

"I'd never think of pressuring you to do something like that. These weeks are about you and whatever feels comfortable for you. Most of the parents are glad to know we have someone looking out for water safety here, but I know that's different for you."

"Yes, it is." Willa forced herself to add, "Thank you for respecting that."

"We've got three whole weeks to figure out what you and the boys want to do. And we're here for you, no matter what that turns out to be."

Whatever it turned out to be, it wouldn't have anything to do with either a photographer or a lifeguard. And it certainly wouldn't be with any man who had the misfortune of being both.

Chapter Two

Later that day, Bruce sat at one of the big round dining hall tables as everyone gathered for their first dinner at camp. Mason had asked Bruce to take all his meals with the camp families every day. It wasn't a hard request to grant, given that nothing much—especially nothing much in the way of good cooking—waited for Bruce at the small house he'd rented down the mountain in North Springs.

The house's large dining room boasted a collection of tables handmade by Mason. He'd felt the large circular tables helped families sit together and get to know each other over meals. Tonight, the room was filled with noisy, bustling activity. Bruce enjoyed the contrast to the bland quiet of his rental place.

A young boy named Marshall Owens stared at Bruce with an awestruck expression. "Mr. Mason told me you jumped out of an airplane," he said as he passed a bowl of spaghetti.

Mason had evidently been talking him up—surely

to keep him from bailing out on account of the Scott-son family's presence.

"Four times," Bruce answered. "And I'd do it again in a heartbeat."

"Cool," Marshall replied. "I'd do it, too."

Marshall's mother gave a mortified expression at the declaration. "Not for at least ten years. And maybe not even then." According to the files Bruce had seen, Marshall's sister had lost her life to a drunk driver as she came home from a high school party. Carol Owens bore a hint of the same ever-watchful caution Bruce was already coming to recognize in all the parents. Mason was right: adding a lifeguard would provide an assurance of safety these parents surely needed.

"My mom hates it when I go off and do stuff like that, too," he said, mostly for Carol's benefit. "She blames me for all the fudge she eats, but I don't think stress fudge is a real thing."

"Oh, it is." Carol nodded. "Very real."

"What else you done?" Marshall asked.

"What else *have* you done," Carol corrected. She directed the next remark at Bruce. "Maybe just the more reasonable stunts, if you don't mind."

He tried to catalog his adventures in terms of mom-safe friendliness. "I've ridden an elephant in India."

"A real one? Like, not at the zoo?" asked Champion Taylor, another young boy across the table, whose mother now bore the same wary-looking expression as Carol Owens.

"Very real, very big." Bruce leaned in, enjoying Champion's wide-eyed curiosity. "And hairier than you'd think."

This seemed to impress Marshall just as much as the skydiving. "What else?"

"I've been to the summit of Denali. That's the highest mountain in North America. Twenty thousand feet— that's four times as high as we are now." He had racked up a long list of daring adventures in the past two years. He'd jumped on every risky and even dangerous photo assignment that came across his desk at the news service. Even he knew that tendency wasn't entirely un- related to what had happened in Florida.

"Whoa," Champion muttered, a forkful of spaghetti halfway to his mouth. "Where's that?"

"It's in Alaska. And it has bears. I got some incred- ible photos of bears," he declared. "From a responsible distance," he added, with a nod toward Mrs. Owens. Actually, he'd been rather irresponsible in how close he'd gotten to one particular mama bear, which gave him a healthy respect for protective moms and the good sense not to reveal that fact at the moment.

"Have you been a scuba diver in the ocean? I wanna do that," Marshall said.

"We did the dolphin experience at the theme park," Marshall's dad, Arnie, offered.

Marshall rolled his eyes. "That's lame."

"You thought it was great at the time," Arnie said.

"I was eight." Clearly, Marshall thought that ex- plained everything, even though the boy couldn't be more than ten at the moment.

Bruce found himself especially aware of Willa's presence at the table just behind him. He sensed her stop moving at the mention of the ocean, as if she were lean- ing over to hear his answer to Marshall's question. In the few short hours of their time here at camp, Bruce had developed a radar of sorts where she was concerned. He needed to know where she was and if she might talk to him at any given moment. Short of that quick exchange in the parking lot when she'd arrived, they'd managed to steer clear of each other. Still, how long would that hold up? Did he stand any chance of making it through the next three weeks without having to talk to her about *it*? The thought of owning up to his cowardice to the woman who had paid the ultimate price for it hollowed out his chest like a cannonball.

"Scuba diving is amazing," he managed to reply, forcing his thoughts back to the present moment. "It's a whole other world down there. Some of my best photos come from underwater. But it takes a lot of training. You have to have the right equipment, and you must learn to respect the dangers."

He was right: Willa had stopped eating behind him. If you could feel someone listening, he could feel her paying cautious attention to him. He was so focused on Willa that he hadn't heard Mason come up behind him.

"Did you know Mr. Bruce has saved someone's life?" Mason asked the family members gathered around the table.

Champion put his fork down even as Bruce felt his gut twist. "No way."

"It's part of the job of a lifeguard," he replied, fumbling through the answer. *And I failed at it. Twice.*

"Was it a shark attack?" Champion blurted out with equal parts fear and fascination.

"No." Bruce shook his head. "Those don't really happen as often as you'd think. Riptides and rough waves pose much more danger to swimmers, even strong swim-mers." Bruce could nearly feel Willa recoiling behind him. He'd heard her husband had been a strong swim-mer. But a storm surge like what had happened to Rick Scottson? Almost no one could have survived it. At least, that's what Bruce kept telling himself... Not that it ever did much good.

"Did they stop breathing?" Marshall seemed deter-mined to press him for details. "Did you have to give them CPR when they'd stopped breathing?"

He really didn't want to get into that. Not with Willa close enough to hear everything. Then again, those fam-ilies needed to know he had the skills to keep them safe. And the camp's little pond didn't threaten any of the risks coastal waters could pose. "Yes. But I hope I never have to do it again." That was certainly the truth.

"What other stuff?" Champion asked. "Tigers?"

Glad to move off the subject of marine dangers, Bruce tried to think up a good but impressive mix of more adventures. "No tigers. A very angry bull, once, though. And three earthquakes—afterwards, not dur-ing. Also, a bridge collapse, an escaped monkey in an airport—that one was hilarious and a bit scary, to be honest—and two forest fires."

The awed looks such a list always generated never sat easily on Bruce's shoulders. He wasn't a hero, even when he had served as a lifeguard. Sure, saving one life was a good thing. But even that would never make up for the two lives he'd failed to save—one of which was the life of the man whose wife and children sat mere feet from him, still trying to climb their way out of the sorrow.

Now Bruce simply tried to be a documenter of heroes. A guy whose job it was to snap pictures of disasters, the people who endured them and the people who fixed them. The high-risk mountain climbs and skydiving? It was coping, not courage. A way to feed the adrenaline rush he seemed to need to fight back the darkness. The real heroes were *in* his pictures—firefighters and bridge builders and first responders.

And today, the people around him trying bravely to put their lives back together after terrible losses—they were a different kind of hero. Next to these people and their struggles, Bruce wasn't a hero at all. Even though he believed in Mason's conviction that the bravery of these people deserved to be told, it felt like some bad joke of Providence that *he* was here.

Bruce fumbled his way through the rest of dinner, relieved when the conversation turned to other topics. By the time the families had gathered outside after the meal to sit around the camp's big round firepit, Bruce was more than ready to leave.

"Good night, Mr. Bruce," Champion called out with a cheery wave. "I wanna go swimming tomorrow."

"Good for you," Bruce said, glad to find a way to put a smile on his face. He'd made it through the first day. It had been far harder than he'd ever dreamed with Willa Scottson here, but he found a shred of pride in the fact that he hadn't backed out…yet.

All the other families chimed in with some form of goodbye and a promise to see him tomorrow…until he walked past Willa, Jack and Joe. An awkward pause hung between them.

"Say good-night to Mr. Bruce, boys," Willa said. He

gave her credit for hiding most of the reluctance in her voice. She looked up at him, the glow of the fire playing across her face, and he was startled to find how pretty she was. He'd seen dozens of photographs of her, had watched that horrible footage of her husband's drowning over and over, but had never seen her in person before today. Not even from a distance. Even now, he couldn't sort through the dozens of reactions he felt in her presence. Fearful and fascinated, like Champion and his shark attacks.

"See ya tomorrow, Mr. Bruce," the boys chimed in tandem. He noticed Willa did not offer the same greeting.

"See you tomorrow, guys." He did want Camp True North Springs to work its healing wonders on this family. In fact, he needed it to. He had to believe God had new, restored lives waiting for those three. He just had to make peace with the fact that he might have to be part of it.

No one bothered Willa with photographs or water sports for the rest of the weekend. It wasn't hard to find "dry land" activities for her, Jack and Joe in the Arizona mountain setting. Chef Seb, who chose a different family to help him make cookies to take to the church service in town, had tapped them for the first Saturday of baking. The chef and his own family had made the whole experience fun. She'd even surprised herself by gathering the twins to attend the church service yesterday morning.

Willa was just starting to think being here wasn't such a bad idea. She sat with her cup of tea on the big house porch after breakfast, as many of the parents did. The food had been wonderful—the boys seemed to put away half their weight in waffles—but the view stole her appetite.

Why hadn't she paid better attention to the camp brochure? When the information said *Arizona*, she'd pictured a cactus-strewn landscape. Half the appeal was that Camp True North Springs would be the farthest thing possible from the surging ocean coast. Water was her foe, the force that had destroyed her life.

And now here she'd spent the entire weekend staring at a pond. Water. Too much of it. She could argue that *any* water was too much water. Not to mention that the camp's nurse, a lovely young woman named Bridget who had recently married the camp maintenance man, handed out water bottles nonstop. Nurse Bridget continually hounded all the campers to stay hydrated. There was a sour justice in that.

Was it petty how much Willa hated the idea of staring at that pond for the next three weeks? Someone else might find it lovely. The pond was thoughtfully framed in her bedroom window. Still, Willa fought the urge to keep the curtains permanently closed or ask to be moved to the other side of the guest barn. But she couldn't possibly move to another room; the twins were too excited about the bunk beds.

What's become of you? She scowled into the amber reflection in her tea. *A thirty-two-year-old woman unsettled by a tiny pond. Don't you dare let the boys catch you like this.* It wouldn't be healthy. It was hardly even reasonable—but what about the grief-filled years had been reasonable?

A thirteen-year-old girl Willa remembered as Nelly

bounded past her chair to skip down the porch steps. "I'm hot. I've been hot since we got here. I can't believe how hot it gets here."

Nelly's mother, Deborah, came out onto the porch. "Aren't you glad we can go swimming anytime we want?"

At least we didn't bring swimsuits, Willa thought to herself. She wasn't sure they even still owned them. With the ever-helpful nature of Dana Avery and the rest of the staff, would that be enough to stave off any invitations to swim?

"I like the pool in our neighborhood better." Nelly wrinkled her nose. "There could be fish in that pond."

"There are," came Charlie's voice as he pushed the screen door open to let himself and the twins walk out onto the porch. "Three kinds."

Nelly clearly wasn't pleased to know the pond was so *populated.*

"I'm swimming with fish? Ick."

A sudden memory of a warm, sunny afternoon invaded Willa's thoughts. She vividly recalled the twin's splashing on the beach, giggling and squealing, "Fishies!" as the waves and saltwater bubbles rushed up against their tiny feet.

The sheer innocent joy of it all pulled at her like an undertow. Those moments felt as if they would never return. The most she could reach for now was a dull, numb existence. Joy was far out of reach. And joy around or about water? Never. That was surely gone for good.

The tea—very good seconds ago—soured in Willa's stomach as she caught the faces of her sons. Joe and Jack made reluctant frowns that matched Nelly's attitude toward the water. Willa had no doubt they'd learned that from her.

"You haven't been swimming yet. Wanna go today?" Charlie asked, as if it were an ordinary, minor thing. "We just put in a ladder off the dock. And you can lie on the new float in the center of the pond and see the clouds for miles."

"Nah," Joe said in a voice that failed to reach the *no big deal* tone Willa knew he was trying to achieve. Some part of her recognized they'd have to find a way to return to the water eventually. She just didn't think it would come up now and be so close. *Couldn't I just start with a kiddie pool? Next summer?*

"Hi, Miss Willa!" Charlie shouted, waving. Willa took encouragement from the boy's exuberance. Charlie had lost his mother in a car crash years ago, and he looked like he was coming out of the grief okay. Mason, too—although everyone gave credit for that to his new wife, Dana, and the camp's mission. Could she hope for that level of healing for Jack and Joe? As to whether or not she could pull off the return to life that Mason had... Well, that felt as far out of reach as the center float sitting in the middle of the pond.

Bruce and Mason came walking up from the water's edge, talking with excitement. "I can't believe that sky this morning," Bruce was saying. "That orange, the sun on the water—great stuff. Took me seven shots, but I think I got it." The animated look on the man's face drained when he saw Willa and her boys. Did she look that sad to people? Wasn't this supposed to be a place where she didn't need to put on the happy mask the rest of the world seemed to demand of her?

Charlie dashed up to his dad and his companion. "Mr. Bruce, Dad told me last night that you can do a flip dive off the dock." Admiration filled the young boy's words. "Can you teach me?"

Bruce put the cap back on his camera lens. "The shore dock's not deep enough for a stunt like that. I'd have to check the depth out by the center float. Can you swim out to there?"

"Sure can!" Charlie declared.

Willa could practically hear Jack swallow hard at the prospect. Her sons looked down at their feet. She sent a silent message to the man: *Don't ask. Don't ask.*

Mason looked at the boys. "It's going to be a hot one today. Sure you wouldn't like to go down by the pond?"

Willa glared at her host. He knew her history. He had to know what an awful question that was. Even Bruce stepped back and lowered his head.

"No." Joe said the word with so much sadness it speared Willa between the ribs.

"I see." Mason sat on the step just below where Joe, Jack and Charlie were standing. "That wasn't an okay question to ask, was it?"

"S'okay," Jack said in a way that let everyone know it wasn't.

"I'm sorry," Mason replied with sincerity. "I promise you, you'll never have to do anything you don't want while you're here."

"I don't want to swim." Jack said it with a dark finality far beyond his years.

Bruce's jaw tightened as if he took that personally. As the camp swimming teacher, maybe he did.

"Do you know how?" Mason asked. "Bruce was just

telling me everyone should know how to swim. It's a safety thing, like knowing your address or looking both ways when you cross the street."

"We used to know," Joe said. "Before."

There was a moment of awkward silence between the adults before Charlie said, "Swimming's fun. I bet you could remember how easy. 'Specially with Mr. Bruce around to show you."

Willa tried to remember that Charlie was just a child. He had no idea the sore point he was making.

"There are lots of other ways to have fun," Bruce offered with an apologetic look at Willa. "You can just look at the water, if that's all you want."

Jack surprised Willa by saying, "I like the sparkles."

"Hey, that's one of the things I like," Bruce replied. "And the way the ripples go out all around. Especially if you throw a stone in some real still water." He reached for his camera, and Willa felt her stomach tighten. He hadn't forgotten her *no pictures* rule, had he? "I threw some stones in the pond a minute ago and took pictures of the ripples. Want to see?"

Willa watched Jack peer into Bruce's camera view screen as the two talked about the water shots. Her son's interest and lack of fear sent a host of emotions through her.

Joe then wanted to get in on the conversation. "You got any pictures of cactuses?" he asked. "Where are the cactuses?"

Bruce managed a small smile. She'd not seen him smile at any point so far, and it surprised her that he had a nice one. Sincere and not overly confident. Most of the media people she'd met were large, invasive personalities with a long string of questions to match.

"That's a really good question, Joe," Bruce said. "You're Joe, right? You two look so much alike. I'm sure I'll get it wrong one of these days."

"Everybody does," Joe said with a mischievous pride. "It's fun."

The boys were fond of playing tricks using their look-alike status. At least, they used to be. Much of the playfulness had gone out of them since Rick had passed—too much of it. Something else Willa knew she should fix. Somehow.

"Well," Bruce said with mock seriousness, "I want the two of you to shake on the promise you won't mess with me like that." He held a hand out to Jack.

Jack shook hands, but Joe balked. "You didn't answer my question about cactuses."

"There are some *cacti* this far up the mountains," Bruce said, emphasizing the correct term. "But the saguaros—the ones I suspect you're thinking of—are farther down into the valley. You'll see a bunch of them when we go to the nature center." He leaned in. "And lizards. And big hairy tarantulas." He picked up his camera again and began scrolling through images. "Here, look. I've got some great pictures of those I can show you."

The next five minutes were spent gawking at Bruce's photos of big hairy spiders, lizards, and any number of things exciting to small—and not so small—boys. It was almost enough to let Willa ease up on her concern…

Until Joe looked at her and said, "Mom, can Mr. Bruce take us swimming tomorrow?"

Chapter Three

Willa scrambled for a way to handle the situation. She fought to keep her composure as she asked Nelly and her mom to mind Jack and Joe for a minute. Then she glared hard at Bruce and Mason and cocked her head at the screen door, a silent demand to step inside and talk out of the boys' earshot.

"Absolutely not!" she whispered harshly the minute they were far enough into the big house. She bit back a torrent of angrier words. "In all honesty, I wouldn't have come if I'd known there would be all this...water." Even she knew how absurd that sounded, but she was so shocked by Joe's question that she hadn't had time to gather her thoughts.

"I'm sorry," Bruce said. "I didn't ask the boys. I wasn't expecting them to ask me. Still, maybe this is—"

She wheeled on him. "Mr. Lawrence, are you aware of how my husband died?" The staff was supposed to be informed of every family's situation.

"I am," Bruce said. "And I'm sorry for your loss.

Truly. I realize swimming might present a challenge for your boys."

"A crossword puzzle presents a *challenge*." Willa narrowed her eyes even as she looked up at Bruce's considerable height. Rick had been a strong swimmer, an athlete like the man in front of her—and what good had it done him against the storm's hungry undertow? "I watched my husband be pulled out to sea. I saw him go under the waves. I never saw him come up. That is not a 'challenge'—it's a horrific tragedy." She felt the tears she never could control rise up at the burden of talking about the worst moment of her life. "The only blessing—if you can call it that—was that the boys were safe in a shelter so they couldn't see what I saw. Can't carry the memories I do. You'll excuse me if I can't quite call that a 'challenge.'"

She was glad to see those words hit Bruce hard, forcing his glance down to the room's weathered floorboards. "I can't come close to knowing what that must have been like for you."

"No, you can't." No one could. Not even all the total strangers who'd watched the news video over and over. It always made her skin crawl to know so many people had been witness to those terrible moments. Why was anyone ever surprised she hated water and despised cameras?

"Willa," Mason said gently, "I do know what it's like to live on the edge of that kind of darkness."

Willa reminded herself that Mason had lost his wife in a tragic way as well, and that he did know the weight of trying to guide a young son through so much grief. Still, she offered no reply.

"Which is why I think we should consider Joe's request."

Willa narrowed her eyes at Mason, surprised he'd even suggest such a thing.

"I get that it's an unsettling thought for you," Mason went on. "But Bruce has a good point—everyone should be able to swim for their own safety. I'd never force them to, but Joe has asked. What if this could be a very safe place to make peace with some of it?"

Her chin jutted out in defiance. "I don't need to make peace with any of it." The moment the statement left her lips, she recognized the absurdity of it. She was afraid of water. Or maybe just living in seething hatred of it.

Bruce surprised her by saying, "You have every right to hate the ocean." For a lifeguard, he made the statement with a surprising amount of understanding.

"But, Willa," Mason added gently, "that isn't an ocean. It's a small, quiet pond. I can't help thinking it's a good place to give your boys back some of what I know the ocean took from them. And from you."

Willa wanted to find Mason's suggestion outrageous. Insensitive. But while it felt quite beyond her reach, she couldn't deny the idea made a frightening sort of sense. It just felt so soon. Two years wasn't enough time to make any sort of peace with Rick's passing. In her heart, the sea had murdered her husband. How could she drop that sword of hatred now?

"I don't know," she said, irritated by the weakness in her tone.

"You don't have to know now," Bruce said. "We have time. I teach lessons every day, and Joe didn't ask for today. The twins can even just watch until they feel ready to join—or not join at all." He paused for a moment before adding, "But Joe did ask. Maybe we owe him a chance."

Willa stared out the window to where she could see the boys on the front porch. She wasn't supposed to have to face this here, now. She'd moved inland after the drowning, but so many mornings, she had considered moving to somewhere as dry as Arizona. Somewhere with no hungry tides and no horrible memories.

This whole weekend had proved that the memories and fear followed her anywhere she went. Rick's death wasn't anything she could run away from—even though she'd been trying for far too long.

She glanced over at Bruce, oddly comforted by the fact that he seemed as bothered by the situation as she was. At least he seemed to realize this was about so much more than swimming. And Mason was right: this did pose probably the safest, most removed setting to deal with the boys' issues over water. It was just a tiny pond, after all.

Willa almost laughed at her own thought. It could never be just a tiny pond to her.

But maybe—just maybe—it could be for the boys. Didn't she owe them that chance? Wasn't healing supposed to be what happened here?

She felt Mason touch her shoulder. "Do you think you could walk over to that tree by the pond with me? Just for a moment? There's something I'd like to show you."

Willa felt ridiculous that Mason had to ask her permission to walk anywhere near water. Even more so that it took such an effort of will for her to agree. She'd grown up on the Atlantic coast. Rick's drowning wasn't the first time she'd known a life lost to the power of the sea. But it was the only time it had felt so horridly personal, so menacing and vengeful. As if the waves would come after her—or worse, the twins—if she gave them the least opportunity. *You're being irrational, Willa.* Still, telling herself that never seemed to help much.

"I'll stand between you and the water, if it'll help." It ought to have sounded condescending, but again, Willa found herself surprised by the compassion in Bruce's gray eyes.

"All right." Willa felt her stomach drop, as if the consent was a leap off some high cliff. "But only if Nelly and her mom will stay with the boys. On the porch. Away from the water."

"Fair enough," Mason agreed. "Give me a minute to check with Nelly and Deb." He pushed back out through the screen door, leaving Willa alone in the front room with Bruce.

For a man of his size and build, he seemed oddly skittish. As if she scared him—which made no sense at all. Perhaps just her insistent demands made him wary of her. Just to cut the tension, she said, "I can't imagine what he could possibly show me."

Bruce looked out to where Mason had been pointing. "Oh, I think I have an idea."

"What?"

"I'll let Mason explain." He almost smiled. Close, but not quite.

True to his word, Bruce positioned himself between Willa and the water as the three of them made their way over to a patch of shrubs off to one side of the pond.

"Over there," Mason said quietly, pointing. "We can't get too close."

Not a problem, Willa thought. "I don't see anything." She was expecting some kind of swimming equipment. Maybe a gigantic life vest or rescue ring.

"There's the mama," Mason said. "Look under that bush. We found the nest two weeks ago. I was worried they'd abandon it over the weekend, with the commotion of all the arriving families, but they're still here."

Willa followed Mason's gesture, scanning the patches of ground under some scrubby brush until she saw it: a mama duck sitting on a nest. It turned its head to look in their direction, and Willa was sure she imagined the protective expression in those tiny round eyes.

She heard a small chuckle from Bruce beside her, who was still putting himself between her and the water. "Seems like not just the humans are going to be learning to swim while I'm here."

Willa turned around to look at him. "You're not going to tell me there's some sort of lesson for me in those hatching ducklings, are you?"

Bruce simply shrugged.

"We'll protect the duck family until the little ones are ready," Mason said. "We'll do the same for you and your boys."

"You have my word." Bruce's words had the solemnity of a vow. "We'll take every precaution and at whatever speed they can handle. It's important to me that I get this right. For you and for them." She might never find another swimming instructor so understanding of her unique situation. He seemed to get what a huge deal this was, whether it made rational sense or not. And the boys liked him. Joe had *asked* if he could swim, after all.

Mason nodded toward the duck family, the brightly colored male now strutting protectively in front of his softer-colored mate and the precious eggs beneath her. "Before you leave, the little guys in that nest will be out in the water."

She didn't care for the *If ducks can do it, so can you* point Mason and Bruce were trying to make. "That doesn't mean I have to be. Or Jack or Joe."

Bruce looked at her, the cautious gaze he'd given her back in the house now replaced by a fierce determination. As if he had something to prove in all this as much as she did. "Maybe it ought to."

Bruce grabbed Dana before all the families filed into the big house for lunch a few hours later. "Did Mason tell you? About Willa and the boys?"

She stopped, still carrying the stack of towels she had been bringing over from the laundry in one of the outbuildings. "I knew just a bit of it before. He told me the rest last night."

"And?" Bruce was half hoping she'd side with Willa and consider the swimming lessons too much for the boys.

"She's been through a lot. So have you. But I think Mason is right—it's no accident that the two of you ended up here. God's up to something."

"What?" Bruce rubbed the back of his neck, sure that whatever God was up to, it was going to be uncomfortable, difficult and painful.

"I suppose we'll have to wait and see. Just let Jack

and Joe set the pace." She started up the porch stairs, and Bruce could hear the ruckus of the families settling down to their meal. "Kids are often way more resilient than we realize," Dana said as Bruce held the door open for her. "Willa has a lot to work through, but Jack and Joe are going to work through it in their own way. If it's swimming for Joe, then I'm glad you're here."

Would he be glad he was here? He couldn't say. He could only say that Willa didn't seem at all sure his presence was a good thing. She looked unsteady and worried every day he'd seen her. The other camp families were relaxing into the session, laughing with each other, talking, making friends. Willa mostly kept to herself.

Bruce purposely sat with Nelly and Deborah Collins, reassuring Nelly that the fish would likely stay away from where he'd set up buoys on the pond to outline a swimming area.

Toward the end of his meal, Bruce felt someone poking him in the back. He twisted in his chair to find Jack, eyebrows furrowed and chin jutting out.

"Hello, Jack. Did you like Chef Seb's mac and cheese today?"

"I'm not going," Jack declared with a surprising seriousness.

He was pretty sure he knew the answer, but Bruce asked, "Not going where?"

"In the water."

Bruce fought the urge to catch Willa's eyes over the head of her son, choosing instead to take Jack at his word. "That's okay."

"Just 'cuz Joe does doesn't mean I hafta."

Bruce pivoted in his chair so that he faced Jack directly. "I agree."

"You do?" Jack seemed surprised.

"Sure. You and Joe are different people. You get to like different things." On impulse, he asked, "What do you like?"

Jack pointed to the backpack slung over Bruce's chair. "Can I see that again sometime?"

"My camera?" Bruce questioned, surprised. "You like my camera?"

The cautious nod Jack gave lodged itself someplace deep and warm in Bruce's chest.

It came to him in a heartbeat. "Would you like to take pictures with me sometime? I can show you how to use it. My teacher used to call it 'going on a photo safari.'"

The boy's eyes lit up at the wording. "Yeah. I wanna go on a photo safari."

"Well, if your mom says it's okay, sure." Bruce welcomed the idea of sharing his skills with the little guy. Especially since he'd made his dead-set-against-swimming opinion known.

"Can I go ask her? Can we go now?"

Now? Bruce had half a dozen things he needed to do before this afternoon's swimming lesson, but suddenly not one of them seemed anywhere near as important as going on a photo safari with Jack Scottson. "Why not?"

The little guy took off with an excitement Bruce felt in his chest. It had bothered him that Joe wanted to swim but Jack still held back. Part of him needed to connect with these boys, needed to do something—anything—that would help them over the massive hurdle life had handed them.

A minute later, Willa walked over to the table, a slightly baffled look on her face. "Jack wants to go shoot photos with you?" Her tone was more startled question than statement.

"A *safari*, Mom." Clearly the word had been the selling point.

"I suppose we can go." Reluctance drew her words out.

Jack's lower lip jutted out. "Not us—*me*. Me and him, Mom."

Bruce had no doubt Willa Scottson was not in favor of letting her son wander the camp with the likes of him. "We could take your mom and Joe with us. We'll all have fun." *Small chance of that,* Bruce thought, catching the scowl in Willa's eyes.

A scowl that was only matched—if not exceeded—by Jack's. "I wanna just go by myself, with Mr. Bruce. If Joe can go swimming without me, why can't I do this without him?"

"It's not my fault you won't swim," Joe moaned at his brother.

Ah, brothers. "That's your mom's call," Bruce said, trying to offer a cooperative glance toward Willa. "We can just stay close to the house and find things to take pictures of there." Why was he so eager for this when ten minutes ago, he was just thinking of all the things he had to do before the swimming lesson?

Jack pouted. "That's not a safari."

"It's not a real safari, anyways," Joe huffed.

Okay, so maybe the word choice hadn't been the wisest. Given Willa's high state of caution, she probably rarely let the boys out of her sight. Bruce hunched down to Jack's height. "A safari can be wherever you find it. Sometimes good photos are of things you think are ordinary, but you take a picture of them in a different way. That's what the best photographers do."

Willa's face softened a bit, so Bruce pressed on. "We'll stay within eyesight. And we won't go anywhere near the pond. You can keep an eye on us the whole time." He straightened up, giving Willa a reassuring look. "Just a half an hour—same amount of time as the swimming lesson Joe'll get." Something told Bruce this small, individual adventure was important, maybe even to all four of them. How had he gone from a man who'd needed to clear off the property when they arrived to someone lobbying for time with Jack?

A long pause stretched between them before Willa said, "Twenty minutes. No pictures of Jack."

Bruce would take the tiny victories where he could get them. "Absolutely. Jack will only take shots, not be in them."

"Why?" Jack asked.

Bruce looked at Willa. How did she explain her banishment of photos to her boys?

"Because I said so." Willa gave her pronouncement a whopping dose of maternal authority.

There's always that. Moms were pretty much the only creatures on the planet who got away with *Because I said so.* This one sure did.

Better go now before she changes her mind. "Okay, Jack, go grab a water bottle and put on some sunscreen while I get some extra gear." He had another camera back in the small closet Dana let him use to store gear. It was a smaller and lighter camera, better suited to

Jack's small hands and sturdy enough to get dropped. "I'll meet you back here in ten minutes."

"Okay!" Jack nearly shouted, taking off toward the stash of water bottles that lined the side of the dining room in a cooler.

It felt good—startlingly good—to see the excitement in Jack's eyes. Bruce had struggled under a press of guilt over these boys for years—a pressure he was sure would never lift, would hound him all his life. Could it really lift, even a little bit? Or was he just fooling himself?

Chapter Four

The afternoon had gone by with an ease Willa hadn't expected. The "safari" had taken place without incident. Jack talked nonstop about his several impressive photos—mostly of rocks and one entertaining lizard—but Bruce didn't push anything beyond that. He hadn't nudged Joe about swimming. All her earlier discomfort had settled down again.

Now it was time for what had become Willa's favorite part of the day: the after-dinner campfire. The heat of the day faded to a pleasant warmth; the children were usually tired out from their activities and sat around the glow of the fire. The older ones talked among themselves or played with the younger ones, so it was one of the easiest times to talk with some of the other parents. Or, like tonight, the younger ones were worn out and near drowsing on cushions or parents' laps.

The indigo sky and slowly appearing stars made the night feel spacious and soft—things life hadn't felt like in a long time. Maybe coming here hadn't been a mistake. Perhaps her friends and pastor had shown some wisdom in forcing her hand to attend Camp True North Springs.

Bruce usually went home right after dinner, never staying for the campfire. But tonight he had stayed, lingering after dinner to laugh with the kids or talk with parents. He'd made a big deal of Jack's photos but had put away his camera for the day. She welcomed not having to watch him out of the corner of her eye. Despite his repeated promises not to catch her or the boys in shots, she couldn't stop herself from keeping her guard up anyway.

She slowly began to sense that he'd stayed to talk to her. He lingered near them until the boys had nodded off, nestled sweetly around each other among big bright blankets on one of the chairs gathered around the fire. He walked over, raising an eyebrow in a silent request to sit in the empty seat on her other side.

"Can we talk?"

Willa still hadn't shaken off the odd notion that Bruce was afraid of her. That was ridiculous, given all the exploits the man regularly recounted to campers. How could she pose any kind of threat to a man who'd jumped out of an airplane or scaled the faces of cliffs? "Sure," she said, in defiance of the wary feeling tingling along the back of her neck.

"I had a load of fun with Jack today. Thanks for letting him do that."

"He had fun, too." Why did that feel so hard to admit? She couldn't quite bring herself to thank him for letting Jack take pictures. Being grateful for something like that still felt a bit beyond her. "What did you want to talk to me about?"

"I wanted to ask you about the boys' history with water. Before your husband's accident."

She was grateful he didn't use the word *drowning*. It always brought up such terrible images. *Accident* was too kind a term—*tragedy* fit what had happened to Rick better—but she'd long stopped looking for the right words to describe that life-shattering day.

"What do you want to know?"

"Did they swim before? Visit the beach, community pools, that sort of thing?"

No one had ever asked her that. Mostly because she'd never permitted the opportunity for it to be any question. She hadn't moved inland for the scenery.

"Yes." Willa didn't like the way it felt like an admission. A confession of how she'd ensured they never went near water now. As if she'd denied them something. Well, water had taken away enough from her and the twins, hadn't it? Who denied who?

"Did they like it? Going to the beach, swimming?"

Again the memory of Jack, Joe and Rick splashing in tide pools and chasing waves invaded her thoughts. "I suppose they did."

"Not every kid does. Some of them start out fearful. Others, well…they learn fear."

Oh, we've learned fear, Willa thought. Some days, it felt like all the reasons to fear water were burned into her heart. "Does it matter?" Or was he just asking out of that morbid curiosity many people—often journalists—seemed to have?

Bruce let out a deep breath and eased back in his chair. "It does, actually." He looked charismatic in the firelight, the flame's glow playing across the strong angles of his face. Women probably found him fascinating—all those heroic exploits and rugged, tanned features. When he was around her, though, a dark edge seemed to come into his eyes. It was so slight Willa wondered if she was just imagining it, projecting her dislike of his profession onto the man himself in order to raise a barrier between them.

"How?" She surprised herself by engaging Bruce in conversation. So far it had been the boys, and rarely her, who pulled Bruce into their meals or activities.

"Having something taken from you isn't the same as never having it at all. Helping Joe re-find his friendship with water is different than showing him how to make friends with water in the first place." He shrugged. "That probably doesn't make much sense to you."

Something taken from you. The words struck her hard. "No, it makes sense."

"Jack doesn't want to get that back yet. And that's okay. But I want to get it right for Joe now that he wants to swim. Helps to know what swimming was like for him before."

Willa looked over to make sure the boys were both conked out. Still, she spoke softly enough that Bruce had to lean toward her. "Joe was one of those kids who would throw himself into the waves, laughing." The words came easier than she'd expected. "Rick called him fearless, which always made me anxious. I felt like I could never turn my back on that boy while we were at the beach."

His smile wasn't a full grin, but held a hint of understanding, as if he'd given his own mother the same kind of grief. It seemed easy enough to imagine, given his endless list of daring adventures. There was something around the edges of how he spoke to her, a caution in how he kept his distance that she hadn't noticed when he interacted with the other families. Not that she'd been watching. It was just that she found her gaze straying to him for inexplicable reasons. To her, the camera in his backpack always clanged like a warning bell. "And Jack?" he asked.

Willa thought for a moment about how distinct the boys' personalities were. On the outside, they were nearly identical. Well, to most people. To Rick and to her—and to those who knew Jack and Joe well—there were dozens of physical differences.

On the inside? It was a whole other story. Jack and Joe sometimes seemed to be the exact opposites of each other. It always struck her as such a marvel. And yes, it showed up in how they treated the water, even before they'd both become fearful of it.

"You know how there are two ways people get into a pool? Those who just jump in the deep end and the ones who ease down the steps in the shallow end?" When Bruce nodded with a smile, Willa continued, "Jack is a shallow-end kind of child. Even before he was afraid of the water, heights scared him. Much more so now." But Rick? Her husband had been a dive-into-the-deep-end man, always gently teasing her about how she eased herself into a pool or the tides.

"I was, too. A cautious kid, I mean."

That surprised her. Bruce definitely struck her as a hurl-himself-off-the-high-dive kind of guy.

He caught her expression. "Guess I've made a career of overcompensating, haven't I?"

"I'd say so." She was startled at the small laugh that accompanied her answer. What must it feel like to blast through your life with all that confidence? She tried to remember the last time she felt capable of any kind of feat. Then again, just getting through some days felt like a massive feat all their own.

Willa wasn't sure what made her ask, "Are you afraid of anything now?"

He paused a long moment before answering. "You'd be surprised." Then, after a long pause, he rose from the chair. "Good night. I'll do my very best to make sure Joe's lesson tomorrow goes well."

Willa hoped that was enough.

It's no different than the other days. He was just adding Joe to the mix—hopefully.

The different ages and experiences in the camp children weren't enough to do separate classes. Still, they were also too different to teach all of them together. Lessons had become a delicate balance of individual attention and group instruction. This first week, especially for the new swimmers, Bruce had insisted that each child have a parent nearby, if not right beside them. For today, Dana had offered to play that role for Joe. That was no guarantee that today's lesson would meet with success for the boy, but Bruce was sure going to try.

He cleared his throat, catching sight of Willa and Jack sitting up on the porch. Jack was curled against his mother while Willa's back was stiff and straight. He admired that she'd chosen to let Joe try today, had told her so last night, and had told her so again today. She was so quick to see her own weaknesses, but he could see her strengths even now. After all, courage was never about the size of the deed—it was far more about the size of the fear. It required no courage for him to climb a mountain because he held little fear of it. Today required a lot of courage from Willa; he knew the size of the fear she battled to let her son anywhere near the water.

"Okay, everyone, let's review the safety rules about swimming."

"We did that yesterday," Nelly said.

"We'll do it every day. It's that important. So who remembers?"

Marshall raised his hand. "Don't go alone."

"Definitely," Bruce replied with a high-five to the boy. "That's rule number one. Never, ever swim on your own. Parents, I'll ask you to abide by the same rule while we're here, even if you're a strong swimmer." He looked around the group. "What else?"

"Don't go too far out," Carol Owens said. "You need to get back."

Bruce nodded. "Absolutely. I know the dock in the middle looks fun, but only those of you who pass my test can have permission to swim out there. Like I said yesterday, it's farther than it looks."

"Stay away from the mama duck's nest," chimed in Charlie. "That's another rule for now."

Not exactly swimming related, but true. "Yes, thanks for reminding us, Charlie. That mama duck and her eggs need us to stay away from them. And if you get too close, I guarantee the father duck will let you know." He'd spent half an hour trying to get some good shots of the duck family yesterday afternoon and had been rewarded with an angry charge and a lot of quacking. *Better than bears,* he thought.

Bruce spent the next thirty minutes reinforcing skills, making sure life jackets fit, coaxing some of the younger ones to put their face in the water—a big first challenge for some of them—and other lessons. He kept his eye on Joe the whole time, aware of how the boy would work up the nerve and then lose it again. In the end, the young boy only watched the lesson, never participating. Dana stayed patiently by his side, offering a perfect mix of encouragement and reassurance.

"You did good today," he said to Joe after the session had ended.

Joe looked at him as if he didn't believe that for a second.

"No, really. This was a big step for you, just being here. I didn't expect you to do anything but watch today, and you did a great job at that." A thought struck him, and he hunched down to Joe's level. "Tell me, do you ever do things without your brother? On your own like this?"

Joe twisted around to look at his mom and brother up on the porch. Willa looked as if it was taking all her willpower not to rush down to the pond's shore and snatch Joe back to safety despite both Bruce and Dana being right beside him. Jack's face held a combination of fear and betrayal—as if Joe's willingness to try swimming was a jab to his young spirit. *I get it, Jack,* Bruce commiserated in his thoughts. *It's hard to watch other people being brave when you feel like a ball of fear.* After being hounded by the thought of ever meeting the Scottson family for so long, Bruce was shocked at the quick emotional attachment he was forming to them.

He was somehow already deeply invested in Jack and Joe's well-being.

He was in Willa's, too. And that felt like dangerous waters indeed. What would happen when she discovered who he was? What he'd failed to do on their behalf?

"Not really." Joe answered the question in a shaky little voice as his chin dipped down and his gaze dropped from his brother. He dug his toe into the sandy soil in a way that made Bruce's heart twist.

"Well, then, today was a really brave thing to do." Bruce fought back an urge to hug the little guy that came up out of nowhere.

"I didn't swim." Joe's lower lip stuck out in a doubt-filled pout as he stubbed his toe into the dirt again.

Bruce sat down beside the boy and patted the ground next to him. "You know what? I'm one hundred percent okay with that."

Joe looked up at him as he planted himself on the grass.

"I am," Bruce repeated. "In fact, I wasn't really expecting you to swim this first time. This is hard stuff."

"Not for Champion."

Champion had, in fact, thrown himself into the water with the fearless abandon Willa had described Joe as once having. Bruce tried to think of a way to recognize Joe's history with water without getting too far into it. It was best to make this about Joe—not about his father's death—as much as possible. In the end, Bruce settled for, "Champion's not you. You're different people. Everybody learns in their own way." Bruce ducked his head down to put his face in Joe's gaze. "But I promise you one thing—we'll find the way that works for you. If you want to swim, I'll stick with you until we figure it out. Even if it takes the whole time you're here. Got it?"

The small spark in Joe's eyes lit a glow in Bruce's chest. Maybe God and Mason were right: maybe the unexpected appearance of the Scottson family in his life really was the way back.

Lord knows he needed one.

Chapter Five

Bruce hit the shutter button and fired off a flurry of shots Tuesday morning. *Gotcha!*

His stomach was sore from thirty minutes of lying nearly flat on the rocky edge of the pond. He was rewarded, however, with a dozen perfect frames of the male and female ducks lovingly touching heads over the nest of their future ducklings. Nature's ideal family waiting to be born. It was as picturesque as his mother's china nativity set. Maybe his favorite shots to date.

He'd had plenty of time to ponder duck familial dynamics while waiting for the animals to get used to his presence and let their guard down. For the first fifteen minutes, the male glared and quacked all kinds of warnings at him. There were a few moments Bruce wondered if today would find him adding *duck attack* to his list of wildlife adventures. Wouldn't that earn him a round of roasting among the guys in the rock climbing club?

Still, there was something about capturing this idyllic animal family. He had an urge to preserve the perfection in the midst of all these broken human families. An internal itch that would not let him give up no matter how much the rocky soil poked his ribs and stomach. Somehow, Bruce knew he would not leave Camp True North Springs until he'd completed a collection of photos of the mallard and his mate, their nest, the eggs hatching, the ducklings growing—all the stages until the victorious moment the brood made it into the pond.

What's happened to me? Bruce wondered as he carefully eased himself up off the stones. For a thirty-five-year-old man who'd spent his recent years photographing large-scale disasters and impressive animals, this made for an oddly small-scale, embarrassingly cute goal. He found himself a bit unnerved by how it had grabbed him and latched on tight.

Rather like Joe and Jack.

Which reminded him, he had a whopping favor to ask of their mother.

Wandering around the camp to find Willa, Bruce ran into Mason working with the camp maintenance man, Carson Todd. They were putting the final touches on the memorial garden that had recently been added to the grounds.

"Make sure you get some shots of this," Mason remarked, gesturing to the rustic wall and the wrought iron arch that framed the entrance to the small garden.

Bruce eyed the structure, noting how the arch lined up with the silhouette of the distant mountains. "If we catch the sunset just right, it ought to be stunning."

That made both men smile. One of the things Bruce liked most about Camp True North Springs was how much pride the staff took in their work. It was compelling, given how his work was starting to sit uneasy on his spirit. He'd never admit to a scrap of envy for the simple, significant life Mason, Dana and the others shared, but it was there—sitting insistent and impatient in the back of his mind.

Mason brushed the dust off his pants as he walked toward Bruce. "Ever done baby shots?"

Bruce stared for a second before asking, "You mean, like portraits?"

"Isabel is thinking about a set of her and Olivia." Isabel was a young widow with a sweet baby girl. "Dana was talking about how she's not had any pictures taken since William died."

The bittersweet request sent a pang to Bruce's heart. "I got some good shots of the two of them on the first day," he offered.

Mason pulled a bandanna from his pocket and wiped his forehead. "Bit different than sitting for a real portrait, I think. Dana sees it as reaffirming that they're still a family even though William is gone. It'd have to be done carefully. 'Compassionately' was the word Dana used." He shifted his weight. "Do you think you're up for it?"

The pang grew into something closer to a calling. "I'd consider it an honor," Bruce answered, his throat tightening a bit with the words. He would. He'd do anything within his power to make things a bit easier for these families.

"I'll tell Dana to talk to her again. We'll see what we can set up." Mason put his work gloves back on. "You were out there by the ducks for a while. Get whatever shot you were looking for?"

Bruce smiled. "I did. Gonna get a whole series, from eggs in the nest to ducklings in the pond."

"Sounds cute," Carson said. "But don't tick off the male. Or the female, for that matter. They don't take well to paparazzi."

Bruce thought about the *Don't mess with me* glare the male duck had given him. "Oh, they made that clear. I'll be cautious. And respectful." He paused for a moment before asking, "Speaking of *cautious*, have you seen Willa this morning?"

"Everybody's over in the vegetable garden this morning. Seb's got some salad project going." Mason gave a smirk. "I didn't ask the details."

Seb was forever inventing ways to involve the families in the camp meals. Bruce would have given anything to be a fly on the wall when Jack and Joe had been on church cookie–baking duty that first Sunday. Those two must have been a handful. "Okay."

"Hope it goes better with Joe today," Carson called out as he started pushing a wheelbarrow toward the workshop behind the barns. "I'll send up a few prayers your way."

"It didn't go very well," Mason commented.

"No, actually, I think it went fine," Bruce replied. "I didn't really expect him to make it into the water the first time. Big leap for a little guy with his issues—and his mom's issues."

"So you want to ask Willa if he's coming back again this afternoon?"

"Actually, I want to ask Willa if she'd be the one to try and make sure Joe comes back this afternoon. It might take some convincing. I think she should do it."

Mason shook his head. "Are you sure she's up to that?"

"No," Bruce admitted. "She's likely to give in way too easily on this. We need to keep Joe from giving up after only one try."

Mason glanced over in the direction of the camp garden. "Tall order. Especially for her."

"No kidding. But, Mason, he wants to. I can see it in him. If we can just get him over his fear—"

"Don't push, Bruce," Mason cut in. "They're all here for healing, not to chalk up victories."

"What if they're the same thing?"

Mason gave him a dubious look. "This from the guy who tried to run from the camp on the first day? You've got a lot of personal stake in Willa and her boys. Maybe too much. Don't make this about your penance when it needs to be about them."

Ouch. Bruce would have been annoyed if there wasn't such a painful ring of truth in what Mason just said. "I don't remember you ever being such a direct guy."

With a smirk, Mason touched his wedding band. "Dana's influence. But I mean it—tread carefully." After a moment, he added, "Does she know? Have you told her how you're connected with what happened to Rick?"

"Of course not," Bruce shot back. "She shouldn't ever know." Panic struck him. "You haven't said anything, have you?"

"I wouldn't do that. It's your secret to tell. But are you sure she shouldn't know? Wouldn't it be better if she did? Less painful?"

"Who are you kidding? She shouldn't ever know. It's better for everyone that way."

If there was one thing Willa Scottson should never know, it was *that*. Right now he was sorry he'd ever admitted it to Mason that one night when he was feeling especially low and his defenses were down.

No. Bruce intended to take that story to his grave.

Willa looked up from unearthing carrots with Jack and Joe to find Bruce standing over her shoulder. "Would it be okay if we took a walk?"

"Now?" she asked. She didn't really want to take a walk with him. "The boys and I are busy liberating carrots." When Bruce raised an eyebrow at the odd term, she offered, "Seb's term. Evidently, it sounds cooler than *harvesting salad*."

As if to prove her point, Jack practically fell over backward as a fat orange carrot came popping out of the sandy soil. "You're free!" the boy yelled as if he'd just sprung the vegetable from jail. The cook was quite the character; that was for sure. But the boys were having fun, so why not?

"Nelly and Deborah said they'd…'liberate'…with Jack and Joe for a minute so we could talk. If that's okay."

She'd wondered when he was going to come and talk about yesterday's lesson. It would take some willpower to bite back the *I told you so* clamoring in her to get out. Still, Bruce had made an effort, and Joe didn't seem too upset by the fact that it had failed. But failed it had. Her heart still ached at the way Joe's head had dipped down as he walked back up from the pond to meet her and Jack on the big house porch. She'd known they weren't ready. Maybe yesterday would put the whole issue to rest for the remainder of their stay here.

Willa waited for Bruce to launch into some explanation or sales pitch about the value of swimming. She didn't think swimming was invaluable—it was; it had been *before*—but she did recognize that it was impossible. At least for now, at least for them. Hopefully, Bruce would recognize that as well.

He motioned toward the back of the property, away from the garden and away from the pond. There was nothing picturesque or special about the expanse of open space back behind the buildings, but it did have the spacious quietness that seemed to fill the camp. All that space made it an easy place to feel small, to hide and maybe to heal. With the exception of the whole swimming thing, Willa had to admit the near-constant twist of anxiety had begun to leave her stomach. There was nothing to prove at Camp True North Springs, no mask of strength to keep on. Everybody could be broken openly and honestly with each other. Maybe coming here wasn't the gigantic mistake she'd first believed it to be. Maybe.

They walked for a minute or so without talking. She appreciated that he made sure the garden was never out of sight, and more than once, Willa turned to check on the boys. They were so preoccupied liberating carrots they barely noticed she was gone.

"Willa is such an usual name," he began. "Is there a story behind it?"

Was that a journalism ploy, or was he truly curious?

"It's not that my parents were disappointed they didn't have a boy they could name William."

He cocked his head. "Do people think that?" He seemed genuinely surprised.

"Well, my dad's name is William. So it's not as far-fetched as you'd think. Dad was actually named after his mother—my grandmother, Willamena. I was named after both of them. That's a mouthful when you're in kindergarten, so I ended up Willa."

Bruce shrugged *"Willamena* sounds…regal, I suppose."

She laughed. When that brought a dubious look from him, she explained, "The reason why neither of the boys is a William is that—" she ticked off on her fingers "—one, you can't really split that between twin boys. And two, Rick was Richard Scottson III and couldn't bear to saddle either of the boys with something like that." Regal indeed.

"Still, I suppose it's nice to have a name with a story—or at least a history—to it."

"Nothing behind Bruce?"

Now he chuckled. "Not a single interesting thing about it."

They'd gone as far from the boys as she wanted to go, so Willa stopped walking and turned to face Bruce directly. "You didn't ask for this walk to chat about names."

One corner of his mouth turned up as he shook his head. "Are you always this direct?"

Willa pushed out a breath. "My life doesn't leave a lot of room for much else. And it's hot." Still, she'd already said more to him than she'd planned to. Was he easy to talk to or just full of those journalism tricks to get people to talk?

Bruce shifted his weight and tucked one hand in the pocket of his very adventure-looking khaki shorts. The man continually looked like a catalog for outdoorsman products—complete with a fit build, tousled hair and a hefty dose of rugged good looks. "I have a favor to ask you. A big one."

That was nervy. "What?"

"I was hoping you'd do everything you could think of to encourage Joe to come to another lesson this afternoon."

Why hadn't she seen this coming? "I can't believe you're asking me that."

He held up a hand in an apologetic gesture. "I get that it's probably the last thing you want. But you should have seen his eyes yesterday. He wants to do this. He just hasn't mustered up enough nerve yet. I don't want to see him fail."

"*You* don't want to see him fail." *You don't have any right to see him do anything,* she wanted to snap back. "I'm his mother. I think this is my call."

"Which is why I need your help. You're the one who will know how to convince him."

Willa didn't bother squelching the mean look she knew was crossing her features. "Why would I convince him to do something I don't think he should do in the first place?"

Bruce straightened. "Because, with all due respect, you're wrong. Joe needs to do this. I know he's only six, and I know I'm not a parent—"

"You're not *his* parent," she snapped.

"I know that. But I make my living observing people, and I can see it clear as day that this represents something to him. Even on his level, at his age. Willa, I think if he fails, it'll stick with him for a long time."

Willa hated even the slightest possibility that Bruce

could be right. Joe had been quiet and sullen since the lesson. More than once today, she'd caught him looking at the pond, staring at the water with something she refused to recognize as longing. It was one thing to work up enough nerve to allow him to try. But to encourage him? To try to keep him from quitting when it was the thing she most wanted?

"I know it's asking a lot," he insisted. "I know I don't really have a right to ask."

"No, you don't."

"But don't you think your boys deserve a victory while they're here?" he went on. "Some small accomplishment to feel good about?"

This isn't small, she wanted to shout. *This is enormous. Far too big. He's just a little boy.*

"I've met a lot of people who've done a lot of reckless running in their lives. Some people run up mountains and dive off cliffs for all the wrong reasons, trying to prove something they should have proven in a much smaller way a long time ago. If I can give Joe that…"

She glared at him. "Why are you doing this?"

He shook his head again. "To tell you the truth, I'm not really sure."

She didn't believe him. No one gives a passionate speech like that and then says they're not really sure. There was something behind why Bruce was putting so much stock in Joe swimming.

Or maybe it was just her overprotective-mother instinct kicking in. Could it really be possible he was just trying to help?

Chapter Six

Joe did not come to the swimming lesson on Wednesday. Nor did Willa agree to encourage him.

Bruce fought his own sense of discouragement. Joe deserved another chance; Bruce just didn't know how to give it to him.

Instead, he tried to be grateful that there was no time for lessons today. Today all the camp families were at the North Springs Nature Center. With the plants in the wild riot of their spring bloom, the lush green and vibrant colors made it the perfect place to get some great shots of the families. In another month, all that growth would fade to brown in summer's sweltering heat, even up here.

He kept his mind focused on the happy victory that had just occurred. Bruce, Dana, Isabel and Olivia had come up an hour earlier than the other families so that they could get a good session of photographs in before Olivia took to napping in the sling Isabel carried her in most of the time. The rugged terrain of both the camp and the center had made a traditional baby stroller impractical, and everyone found the sight of Olivia snuggled up against Isabel charming.

Both mother and daughter required extra care at first—handling that was much more about who *wasn't* in the photograph than who was. There was a lot of grief to wade through at first, but the shots toward the end were sweet and tender and downright heartwarming. Now, walking along the trail behind the other families, Bruce found himself smiling as he recalled a frame of Olivia reaching one tiny hand up to touch her mother's cheek.

A high-pitched yelp caught his attention. Bruce looked up to see Willa grasping at Jack and Joe, taking small but rushed steps backward and away from something.

He stashed his camera in his backpack the way he always did around them and dashed forward. Willa nearly crashed into him as she continued edging her way back down the path. She yelped nearly as loud at their close contact as she had cried out at whatever had sent her down the path.

Bruce grabbed her shoulders for a second to keep her and the boys from tumbling over, as she had the two of them clamped to either side with an iron grip. "What's wrong?"

She stayed pressed up against him as she pointed a few feet up the path. "That!"

Bruce followed her gesture and found a smallish tarantula standing in the path. Frozen, he could guess, by the shriek of the tall being that had come across him on the path.

"It's huge." Willa's voice was a mix of squeak and whisper.

"He's more afraid of you than you are of him," Bruce said. *Him*, because the size told Bruce it was a male. The females were much larger, but he didn't think that was the sort of fact he ought to share right now.

"I doubt that," Willa said.

"He's hairy," Joe said with a hint of wonder.

"He's looking for his lady spider. She's probably over there, somewhere in her den."

Willa started backing up against Bruce again, but something in him said to hold steady. "It's okay. Just give him a minute."

"I don't want to give him a second." Willa squinted her eyes shut. Bruce felt her lean a bit against him.

"You don't have to be afraid of him," Bruce said in a low, reassuring tone. "He only looks scary. He's using the path, just like we are."

"Will that big spider bite us?" Joe said, squeaking a bit himself. Bruce felt Joe's arms clamp around his leg.

He put his arm on the boy's shoulder. "He's called a *tarantula*. And he won't bite you unless he thinks you're going to hurt him. People have held them. Some people even keep them as pets." That brought a mortified groan from Willa and Jack. "I don't personally recommend it," Bruce said. "Everyone's better off with them living out here."

"Have you held one?" Jack asked, looking a little too intrigued.

"Once," Bruce admitted. "That was enough for me. But just stay still for a moment and let him walk away. It's actually pretty neat how they walk."

"I'd rather he run away, thanks," Willa said.

Maybe it wasn't just Jack and Joe who needed a little

victory of courage while they were here. "Don't turn back now. Everyone else is farther down the trail. Just stay for a minute and let him pass." When Willa gulped loud enough for Bruce to hear, he added, "You can do this, Willa. He's not going to hurt you or anyone."

He was glad that Willa didn't turn and run. He kept his hand on Joe's shoulder and, after a moment, put his other hand on Jack's as well. He didn't dare touch Willa but was glad she stayed right there, pressed against him fiercely enough that he could hear her short, tight breaths.

Everyone stood still. After half a minute, Willa squeaked, "Why isn't he moving?"

"He's as worried as you are. Oh, wait, look—there he goes." The black-and-brown spider moved one leg, then another, then slowly made his way across the path. He sped up in a flurry of furry legs and disappeared under the brush.

Willa softened against him, bringing her hands up to cover her face as she let out the breath he knew she'd been holding. Bruce dared to put a hand on her shoulder then. "He's gone," he said, surprised at the tenderness in his own voice.

He looked down at the boys. "Your mom was very brave just then. You too." Pronouncing their courage set a small glow under his ribs.

"I don't think so," Willa said, taking her hands off her eyes and giving him a dubious look he found, well… endearing.

When did he become the kind of man who found things *endearing*? *Compelling*, maybe, but *endearing* was a whole other kind of thing. "Yeah, you were," he encouraged her, the tentative look in her eyes snag-ging some long-forgotten part of his spirit—a pull that made him glad he hadn't bolted that first day. "You did something that scared you. That's my definition of being brave."

"I didn't do anything."

A smile came so easily it surprised him. "Just the point. You wanted to run, but you didn't." The truth that the words applied to both of them struck him deeply. "Sometimes, I think the hardest thing to do is to do nothing. Just stick where you are, and take in what the world is showing you." He tried a bit of bravery himself, adding, "What God might be showing you."

Willa nearly rolled her eyes at that. "There are no spiritual truths in tarantulas."

"Tarantulas!" Jack said, making spider legs at his brother with his fingers. The boy clearly found the word entertaining. Joe did roll his eyes, seeming to find his brother's enthusiasm annoying.

Bruce had to laugh. Foreign as it felt in his chest, he felt something loosen a bit. As if being near Willa Scottson and her boys wasn't the difficult challenge he'd feared it would be.

Still, that was because they didn't know. The grow-ing friendly glow between the four of them would pop like a bubble—or maybe explode like a bomb—if he revealed the truth. The most he could hope for was to help them along their path while he was here. This one today and the larger one of their grief and healing. That would all end when the camp session was over, and that was for the best.

So much of him wanted to capture the look Willa

gave him as he motioned for them to move forward on the path. Her eyes held gratitude, doubt, a spark of friendship and the fierce strength he knew she thought she'd left behind. He yearned to photograph that look—the tilt of her chin, the way the sun made the green of her eyes practically glow.

He'd have to make do with his memory of the moment. And somehow, he knew the image of her expression would stay with him just as long as if he'd caught her on film.

Willa sat with Vanessa Taylor in rocking chairs later that afternoon, watching Jack, Joe and Champion play some sort of made-up spider game on the patch of grass in front of the big house.

Vanessa was working yarn and needles into what looked like a scarf—a surprising choice of garment, given the stifling heat. Still, it looked like a soothing activity. Knitting in rocking chairs felt like the sort of thing grandmothers with a lot of free time did, not stressed-out, grief-laden single moms.

"How do you find time to do that?" Willa asked as the boys shouted and scurried from one side of the grass to the other.

Vanessa's laugh was deep and rich. "I don't. I started this as a Christmas present last year. I don't know what made me put it in the suitcase. I mean, it's upwards of ninety here."

Willa pointed to the deep red of the yarn. "It's a beautiful color."

Vanessa held up the long strip of stitching and admired it. "This was Forest's favorite." She waved the scarf. "*Roll tide.* We met at college in Alabama. 'Course, everyone who didn't understand football thought his favorite ought to be green, given his name and all." She shook her head and gave a short amused hum. "That man never did take to what other people thought he ought to do."

Willa recognized the flash of love and loss in the woman's eyes. "How did you lose Forest?" There was something deeply healing in the fact that she could ask that question here. Everyone else knew how sharing the story helped and didn't get that *Are you sure we should be talking about this?* look so many of Willa's friends got whenever she told stories of Rick.

Vanessa let the knitting fall to her lap. "Hit-and-run. I wish I could say it was something important—something heroic like a firefighter or a soldier—but it was just the stupidity of someone running a red light in a stolen car. We never did find out who did it." She gave Willa a weary look. "Not everyone gets justice, you know?"

Willa sighed. "I do. You can't arrest the ocean for murder."

Vanessa's wide brown eyes went wider. "Your husband *drowned*?"

"Right in front of me." Some days, those words ripped their way out of her; other days, they just fell out numbly. Today she wasn't sure which it was.

Vanessa's rocking chair stilled, and she put her hand on Willa's arm. "And your boys? They saw their daddy drown?"

"No. That was the one blessing of it. They were in a shelter. I can't imagine what seeing that would have done to them."

"I can't imagine what seeing that did to *you*."

Willa shut her eyes for a moment as the scene replayed itself in her brain. Someday she hoped to be able to stop that flashback from coming up on her like that. Perhaps years from now, it wouldn't hit her with the force of ten hurricanes. Then again, maybe not. It was the last time she saw Rick, after all. It'd be wrong to forget that, no matter how much it hurt.

"I get the water thing now," Vanessa said. "I saw Jack staying on the porch. And my heart broke at how Joe couldn't get himself off the shore at the lesson." Vanessa's lilting southern accent held a tone of warm understanding. "Mercy. You probably couldn't get me near a bathtub after what you've been through."

Willa could almost laugh. "My sister thinks I'm overreacting." After a pause, she added, "Almost *everybody* thinks I'm overreacting."

"I don't think so," Vanessa replied. "It's been three years, and I still can't make it into a crosswalk without my pulse jumping to the sky. Someone had to practically hold me down to let Champion cross the street on his own for the first time. And that was with a crossing guard and a whole bunch of older kids all around him." The woman started rocking again, returning to her knitting. "No, sir, I don't think anyone can tell you how to get through this. Certainly not anyone who hasn't been through it."

It felt so good to hear someone tell her she wasn't losing her grip. She glanced at the boys, who were playing happily and far away from the pond. "I told myself to stay up here on the porch while Joe was down there. My heart was about to pound out of my chest the entire time. I kept wanting to run down there and snatch him back to safety—but at the same time, I couldn't bring myself to go near the water."

Vanessa turned a row on the scarf. "That's no way to live. Surrounded by all that fear."

She seemed so much calmer than Willa. "How did you get past it?"

"Who says I'm past it?" Vanessa laughed. "I paid the extra fee so Champion could ride the bus to school from his day care." When Willa gasped in surprise, she added, "I figure it was that or my nerves. You cope where you can, right?"

Willa had done so many things she considered silly or unwise just to get by. She had single mother friends, but none had been widowed at a young age, with not one but two rambunctious boys to manage. Vanessa's laugh and teasing eyes were a balm to her ragged spirit. She let her head fall back against the rocking chair, feeling something close to peace for the first time in a long time.

The two mothers watched their trio of sons shout and scurry, enjoying their fun. After Jack yelled, "Tarantula!" again, reprising his endless fascination with the word, Vanessa leaned in and asked, "Did you really face down one of those big hairy spiders at the nature center? I saw the sign in the visitors' center saying to be on the lookout for them, and it gave me the creepy-crawlies while we were out on those paths."

"'*Face down*' might be overstating it," Willa admitted. "I'm not even sure I can truly say I didn't run away, because I would have if Bruce hadn't been there to stop me."

"I was so busy watching for spiders I'm not sure I really saw any of the plants. Champion is actually jealous of the boys, but I'm just fine with skipping that adventure."

"I would have preferred to skip it, too. I'm glad Bruce was right behind us, even if it did mean he heard me yelp."

"Good man to have around, that Bruce. Big and strong. No spider would be a match for him. Seems nice, too. Patient with the kids."

"Seems so." He was. Bruce had had so much concern in his eyes when he asked Willa to try and convince Joe to come back for another lesson. He'd had so much compassion in his eyes when he steadied her on the nature center path. She felt…something…being that near to him. A connection, an awareness… Certainly nothing she could or would consider attraction. Sure, opposites attract, but you couldn't get further from her cautious personality than Bruce Lawrence.

"I was watching the way he reacted when Joe wouldn't go in the water," Vanessa offered. "I know plenty of men who would get all 'buck up and get in the water, son,' but he didn't. You wouldn't think that of a man with his experience, all rough and rugged. But there's something else about him, don't you think?"

There *was* something else about him. Willa just wasn't ready to discover what that was.

Chapter Seven

Bruce stood by the towels spread out next to the pond on Friday afternoon. He was getting ready for the day's swimming lesson—or at least, that's what he was supposed to be doing. Mostly, he was staring at the door of the barn where Willa and the boys were staying, praying they would walk through it on their way toward him. At least just Joe, although he hoped Willa would come even a little bit closer this time. She'd stayed up on the porch last time, as if the Grand Canyon stood between her and the pond. Even from here, he had seen how her hands gripped the porch rail.

Did he have any right to ask her one more time to try to convince Joe to come back to the lessons? Sure, he firmly believed swimming was important for safety and confidence. Still, this was no ordinary swimming lesson. Jack and Joe were no ordinary boys. And Willa was certainly no ordinary woman.

I need Your help here, Lord. I'm in over my head. Too true a choice of words for his situation.

Ten minutes before the lesson was scheduled to start,

just as the other kids had started gathering, Bruce saw the barn door open. The tight band around his chest loosened when he saw Joe in swimming shorts. He was clutching Willa's hand, but Bruce could see the pint-size determination in those green eyes. *That's it, kid—try again. You can do this. I'll be right here for you.* Followed by a humble, heartfelt, *Thank you, Lord.*

Bruce smiled and waved—but not too much—as he met the boy's gaze. Without his asking a second time, she'd convinced Joe to come back. Willa Scottson was braver than she gave herself credit for, and he made a mental note to make sure he told her so the next chance he got.

His smile broadened when he noticed her take a few tentative steps down off the porch. She hadn't ventured off it last time, and he took the closer distance as a big win. He walked toward her and the boys, feeling a glow of satisfaction as she settled herself and Jack onto one of the benches that dotted the lawn.

"Hey there, Joe. Glad to see you back again."

"Yeah." The boy's tone was unsteady, his eyes darting back and forth between his mother, Bruce and the pond behind them.

There were a million things Bruce wanted to say to Willa, but it was wisest to play this moment down for now. They could celebrate when Joe made it into the water—*if* he made it into the water today. Bruce hadn't yet worked out what he would do if he failed to get Joe in the water again today. He wasn't sure there'd be another chance. In the end, he gave Willa a knowing smile and a small nod, then surprised himself by offering Joe a hand. "Want to come sit on the edge while we wait for the other kids?"

"Okay."

Together they walked to the place where the pond met its bank. Bruce sat down with his feet stretched out into the pond, his long legs crossing a strip of sand between grass and the tiny waves the breeze was stirring up on the water. The pond was near perfect—refreshingly cool but not uncomfortably cold. Without a word, he waited for Joe to choose his position.

Joe sat on the grass but settled himself right up against the sand, toes lining up inside red rubber sandals. He hugged his knees to his chest, a little ball of anxiety reaching for courage. The urge to put his arm around the kid was powerful, but Bruce played it calm and casual.

Bruce leaned back on his elbows, a move that put his face close to Joe's height. "Water's nice today. Good day for a lesson."

"Uh-huh."

"I'm glad you're here." It seemed like the right thing to say. And he was glad Joe was willing to give things another try. Bruce had been unable to shake the sense this was a pivotal moment for Joe, Willa and maybe even Jack.

Joe stared at the water and wiggled his toes. Maybe wondering how those toes would feel in the water?

"Got any questions?" Sometimes when he taught swimming, the questions kids would ask told him a lot about their fears and worries.

"Can spiders swim?"

He wasn't expecting that one. "I don't actually know. What do you think?"

Joe shrugged. Bruce noticed the boy's toes wiggled just a small bit onto the sand. Some victories were won in fractions of an inch.

"Well, lots of bugs hang around the water or on top of it. I expect somewhere in the world, there are spiders who can swim, but I don't think any of them are here." He tried a tactic, nodding his head back toward where Willa and Jack sat. "Is your mom worried about spiders in the pond?"

"Sorta." It didn't take much to realize Joe's answer wasn't really about his mother.

"But your mom was brave yesterday, wasn't she? With that big spider and all."

"S'pose."

"I think you can be brave, too." Much as he was pulling for the boy, Bruce felt like he had to add, "If you want."

Joe turned to look up at Bruce. "I wanna. But it's scary."

Bruce shifted to face the boy. "I know it looks that way—and it feels that way. But it doesn't have to. It can be lots of fun. Your mom told me you used to have fun in the water."

Joe chewed his lip, a gesture that tugged hard at Bruce's heart. If there was any doubt he wasn't absolutely invested in this family's return to the water, it was long gone.

"You can have fun again. It might take a while, and it might feel hard at first—but, Joe, I gotta tell you, I know you can do this." The conviction in his own words caught Bruce by surprise, but he meant every one of them.

Getting an idea, Bruce pulled his knees up to mirror

how Joe sat. "How about we play a little game about it before the other kids get here?"

Joe thought about it, the decision playing seriously across his small features. *Just a small win here, Lord. That's all we really need,* he prayed as he waited for the boy's answer.

"Okay."

The one small word ignited a fierce hope in Bruce's chest. He shuffled a little closer to Joe. "Here, line your toes up with mine."

The boy planted his two feet so that they sat at the edge of the sand. Making a big show of it, Bruce moved his left foot half an inch toward the water. He pointed to Joe's left foot. "Now yours. Just a bit."

Bruce practically held his breath while Joe hesitated, then pushed his foot across the grass to meet Bruce's. Those green eyes looked up at Bruce, and Bruce wondered if this is what it felt like to have your heart melt.

He shifted his other foot to match the first one. "Now the other one."

Joe followed suit. When Bruce gave a small laugh, Joe managed a bit of a giggle.

Back and forth, back and forth, the two sets of feet scooted in tiny bits until Bruce felt the water lap at his toes. Wondrously, Joe's toes did the same. Within a few minutes, both pairs of feet were in the water, and the small giggles had turned to full laughs.

Bruce leaned in. "Wanna splash?"

Joe's eyes widened as if splashing was breaking all kinds of rules. In response, Bruce tapped one foot against the water, sending a little ripple across their feet. He could see the idea bubble up through Joe, bursting out in the form of a big kick that sent droplets across the both of them. Within seconds, the two were kicking and splashing and laughing so loud that several of the other families turned to look.

Even Willa. Her expression of fearful delight felt as if it would stay with him forever.

Of all the big daring feats Bruce had done, this small one wasn't small at all.

Joe was in the water.

Not all of him, of course—just his feet and whatever part of his legs were being splashed by his antics with Bruce. Still, it was a huge thing—Joe was in the water, and she had not come undone. She could, for one small moment, come close to being happy for her son. There, making silly noises at the edge of the pond, was a picture of healing. Just the very beginnings of healing, but somehow that seemed enough.

"Will you look at that?" Isabel said as she sat with baby Olivia in the shade.

Willa had too much emotion piled up to let any words pass her throat. She managed a nod and a small hum, but nothing more than that.

She turned to see Jack's reaction to the splashing taking place. Her son shot a quick glance down to his brother by the pond and went back to the trucks he'd been zooming across the grass. It didn't take a mother's intuition to see the war going on inside her son: part of him wanted to be like Joe, to go near the water. But the larger part of him wasn't ready.

"You don't have to swim just because Joe is," she

assured him quietly. He wasn't ready. She knew a lot about not feeling ready.

"I don't wanna," Jack muttered.

Willa watched the lesson, her heart in her throat. She observed the steady patience Bruce showed not only Joe but every child. He met their eyes. He talked to them, not at them. He joked and laughed, handing out high fives and smiles with an astounding generosity.

Bruce Lawrence had changed from the man she'd met in the camp parking lot a week ago. Before, he'd simply been an obstacle, a source of caution and worry. Someone to be avoided, someone to keep at a safe distance.

Now he was almost an ally, a strong and solid person she could trust with her sons. Hadn't that been what she'd prayed for in coming here? Someone to do the job of guiding the boys to healing in a way that she couldn't? Ah, but they were a long way from healed. And truly, could she really hope for anything more than coming away from this time anything more than "a bit less scared"?

"Can you believe that man threatened to leave on our first day?" Dana asked as she came out from the big house and stood behind Willa and Isabel. "That man is right where he's supposed to be, doing exactly what he's supposed to be doing."

"Sure looks that way to me," Isabel agreed.

Dana sighed. "I always say God brings the right people to Camp True North Springs. We send out materials and such, but it's God who sends the campers to us."

"Didn't you say your church sent you here?" Isabel asked as she shifted Olivia to her other shoulder.

"They did." Willa looked up at Dana. "I wasn't very happy about coming, if you hadn't noticed."

Dana gave a smile. "Really?" Of course she'd known Willa hadn't wanted to come; she'd been downright grumpy those first days. Still, there was no judgment in the camp director's eyes. "And how do you feel about it now?"

Just as she finished the question, Joe came barreling up toward Willa, throwing himself into her lap, wet legs and all. "Mama! I put my toes in the water! I splashed Mr. Bruce, and he splashed me right back."

Bruce came up a few paces behind, his grin matching Joe's. "We had fun, didn't we?"

"Yup." Joe looked into Willa's face with happy eyes. "I'm wet," he proclaimed.

Willa found she could actually laugh. "Yes, you are."

"Best wet ever," Bruce said with a laugh. The man looked as if he held the victory as dear as Willa did. While only Joe's legs were wet, Bruce was soaked from head to toe. Part of that was because he had finally given in to Charlie's request to do a backflip off the center dock. It was quite the spectacle. She had to admit, Bruce was athletic and daring…and no small amount of handsome.

Willa held his gaze for a moment, then turned to Dana. "I'm glad we came."

Chapter Eight

Bruce moved the camera a few inches to the left and adjusted the exposure. *There it is.* The silhouette of the tree branches perfectly framed the little garden, with its stone wall and metal archway sitting below sparkling strings of lights. The sky was the deep indigo of a new night, a rich color that only appeared just before the stars came out. A few of the dozen shots he snapped surely had to be perfect, if not all. There was so much beauty in this place that he found it was almost an act of worship to capture it on film.

A noise behind him made him turn around. Willa walked cautiously into the soft circle of golden glow the light strings cast onto the paving stones. "Am I interrupting?"

He was delighted to see her. And while that was perhaps more emotion than was wise, given their circumstances, Bruce seemed unable to stop it. He still hadn't stopped thinking about what it'd felt like to come up out of the water toward her, glowing with the knowledge that he'd helped Joe wade in a bit and splash. "No. Not at all."

"Jack and Joe are conked out from the Saturday hike. Deborah and Nelly offered to sit with them so I could take a walk—well, *another* walk." She said it as if she needed to explain her presence. After all, a walk after a long hike was a bit…redundant.

He didn't mind at all. "It's a gorgeous night. This bit of time—after the sun sets but before the stars come out—is always my favorite." He stowed his camera the way he always tried to when she was around. His usual bulldozer-of-a-guy-thrashing-through-life impulses somehow dissolved around her, replaced with a strange need to be… Be what? *Tender* was the word that came to mind, but that seemed all wrong.

He sat on the low wall, a nod of his head silently inviting her to do the same. It made him happy that she did. She had seemed so uncomfortable—threatened, even—by his presence those first days at camp that every bit of comfort she showed now touched him. Made him feel as if perhaps he hadn't destroyed her life after all.

"I can't decide if I want to thank you or be mad at you."

If Willa was anything, she was honest and direct. "Maybe we go with the first choice?" Still, he understood what she was saying: things were far simpler if they were adversaries, more complicated as allies.

"Joe is so proud of himself. You'd think those two feet in a few inches of water were the greatest thing in the world."

"It is—to him, right now, at least. Facing a fear—two inches of water or a big hairy spider in your path—is an enormous thing. He should be proud."

Willa gave a small chuckle. "Oh, he is. Won't stop talking about it, which is starting to get on Jack's nerves. They're bickering, so this walk isn't entirely just for sightseeing."

He wanted to encourage her. "You should be proud, too. I know I asked a lot of you to nudge Joe back to the pond. It wasn't hard to see what a challenge it was for you to watch him." Bruce picked up a small rock that someone had placed on the wall—a smooth one still a bit warm from the day. He turned it over in his hands, running his fingers along the curves of it. When was the last time he'd skipped stones on the flat surface of a calm pond? When was the last time he'd done anything so peaceful sounding? "Courage of one kind always makes courage of another kind possible. It's never just about swimming."

She shot him a sideways glance. "Yes, well, now I have a little boy who wants to go farther into the water next time. What am I supposed to do about that?"

The answer was both easy and impossible. "Let him?" Bruce offered.

Willa looked up at the sky, where a few stars had started to appear. "Easy for you to say."

"I'll watch over him, Willa." It was the first time he'd called her by name, and it stuck in his chest in some deep and important way. Still, it felt like too much to say something like *You can trust me*. Because, of course, she couldn't.

"What do I do when Jack wants to join him? What do I do when they dive under the water? When my heart stops because I'm not sure they'll come back up again?"

She turned to look at him with raw grief in her eyes. "How do I do that?"

Every inch of him stung from the sharp edges of her tone. He had been sure he recognized the depth of her loss before now, but he was wrong. It went so much deeper than he knew—than maybe he could bear. And yet Joe had put his toes in the water—literally— and there seemed to be no going back from whatever came of it.

Half out of self-punishment, half because he didn't know what else to do, Bruce said, "Tell me about that day." There was no need to say what *that day* was and no guessing how much it would hurt to hear. No matter what he'd imagined, it could only be far worse from her point of view. He owed it to her to listen, to give her the chance to recount the worst moments of her life to him.

And while it would destroy the perfect beauty of the night, Bruce knew this might be the only chance he would get to hear the story he most dreaded to hear.

Tell him? About that day?

Willa didn't think she could do it. Honestly, she tried to avoid speaking about it to anyone. At all costs. It just brought everything back to the surface. Even the few sentences she'd given Bruce and Mason felt like too much.

And yet it did make sense to tell him. She needed him to know. She expected Bruce had a vague idea of what Rick's drowning had done to her, how it had torn her life apart.

People always *thought* they knew. They said irritating phrases like, "I know how you must feel." But *no one* could know what it had felt like to watch Rick go under. The pure dread that had iced over her when he did not surface. And did not surface. And never surfaced again, except as a body the Coast Guard had told her was "better not to see." Rick's boss had offered to go identify the body, and Willa always felt that was the bravest and kindest thing anyone had ever done for her.

So she asked the true question: "Do you really want to hear it?"

She tried not to make it sound like a challenge, but in Willa's experience, few people really wanted to hear the harrowing story. That, plus a desperate need to keep the flood of emotions down where she could control them, kept her silent.

Bruce's "Yes" was simple and determined. That surprised her. It pulled up some deep and long-ignored urge that was stronger than the sadness. How would it feel to know one other person here understood the full weight she carried? He ought to know. He ought to be made aware of it—after all, his own words had been "It's never just about swimming."

Willa looked down at her hands, finding the air too thin and the space too wide. *Start. Just start.*

"It was the big hurricane—the one that changed direction so quickly the evacuation orders didn't come fast enough. We had sent the boys inland, to a friend's house the day before, just to be safe. That turned out to be such a blessing."

"I'm sure," Bruce said. His voice was low and soft.

"But we'd just redone our home, and it had all the storm-safety upgrades. Rick felt we'd be safe riding it out, and he was worried about looters and damage." She looked at him, wanting him to understand that it hadn't been a foolhardy decision. They hadn't ignored warnings, and the house had withstood the storm. That was the hardest thing to understand—her life had been shattered, but every dish was still in its place in the kitchen. She was a widow, but the house looked as if nothing enormous had happened.

"We thought the worst of it had gone through. It had been bad, the hours before, but it was letting up. It looked safe to go outside. Not pleasant—the rain and wind were still gusting a bit—but not unsafe. He wasn't being reckless. People don't seem to understand that."

Bruce nodded but didn't reply. He was listening. Still, she could tell the story made him uncomfortable. It was a painful story—how could it not?

At first, Willa thought she might start to cry, but it was as if she'd moved a distance from herself, as if some other woman was making her way forward through the traumatic facts.

"It was the car, if you can believe it. We'd bought a new car three weeks before, and a huge branch was dangling off the tree above it. 'I'll just go move the car,' he said. 'Now, while it's let up a bit.'" She could hear his voice, how ordinary he'd made the task sound. "'Be right back,' he said."

She remembered looking down from the big windows that let out onto their balcony, able to see through them clearly after hours of being blurred by wind and rain. "There were other people out there. A van from the local television station had pulled up a handful of parking spaces away from our car. They had started filming. Of course, we all know they didn't stop filming, don't we?"

That was the question that would follow her to her grave. Why hadn't they stopped filming? Even when it had turned horrible, why hadn't they stopped filming?

"He was just turning around to come back to the house from moving the car..." A spike of anger surged through her, and Willa balled up her fists. "The stupid, replaceable car. The not-worth-his-life car that ended up swamped by the same wave anyway." She remembered the way he'd looked up and waved to her on the balcony just before, the way he'd caught the look on her face as Willa realized the water was rising to rush up behind him.

"When the wave came—and it came out of nowhere, rising up out of nowhere—I ran out onto the balcony. I yelled to them. I begged them to stop filming and help him." Now the distance fell away, and she felt far too close to the story again. Willa looked up at the dark sky, reaching for the courage Bruce claimed she possessed. The courage seemed out of grasp, and she couldn't find the next words.

Bruce found them for her. "They didn't."

They were horribly sad words. Tragic and avoidable. If only they had made a different choice, the choice Willa felt any compassionate human surely would have made.

"They said it was unsafe. That it wasn't their place to try and rescue him. 'We are journalists, not lifeguards,' they said. Oh, they kept saying how terrible it was and how sad they were, but they weren't sad enough to put down their camera and help my boys' father. My husband."

Bruce closed his eyes. "I'm sorry. I'm so sorry."

So many people said that to her. Most of them meant it, but only in a polite kind of way. Willa was touched by the way Bruce seemed to truly mean it.

She pivoted on the wall to face him. "I should have run down there. It was like I couldn't move. I couldn't take my eyes off him. I couldn't believe they wouldn't drop their equipment and go out to help him, even when I screamed at them to help."

"I can't imagine. They should have helped. Any decent person would have. I would have." His voice cracked on those words. "If I had been there, I would have helped."

All the *would have*s and *should have*s—she'd been living under the weight of them for years. "You were a lifeguard. That's different, I suppose. But they tell me they would have needed someone on a Jet Ski or in a boat to have pulled him from that current." She heaved in a breath. "Even I couldn't help him. I couldn't even make myself try to run down there because…because I thought if I took my eyes off him for one minute, he'd be…he'd be gone." Willa felt the weight of that moment wash up over her again. "And then he was." She wiped tears from her cheeks, glad for the dark around her to hide how raw and cracked open she felt. "I didn't even see his face that last moment, just the back of his head. Slipping under." It still stunned her how such a gray, wet moment could burn through her like fire.

There was a long moment of mournful silence. Willa wanted to hang on to something, to someone, before it took her under, but this wasn't the time or place. Instead, she hugged her arms to her chest. She noticed—with an odd sense of victory—that while she was crying, she wasn't sobbing.

"You know, that's the first time I've told that to anyone without going totally to pieces." She noticed out of the corner of her eye that Bruce's hands were in tight fists, his breath coming in short spurts. Maybe he really did understand the anguish of watching someone succumb to the waves. He had boasted at that first dinner about saving a life. Had he ever failed? While his reaction made her think maybe so, Willa didn't have the composure to ask him right now. Instead, she just let the warm silence of the night pull them both back from the brink of so much sadness.

He spoke first. "I'm so, so sorry." Bruce's voice was broken and ragged. It seemed wrong to take comfort in their shared sorrow—but these days, Willa took comfort anywhere she could get it.

It was pointless to try to talk about anything ordinary now. And she was suddenly exhausted, needing to go find the boys and hug them tight. "I should go," she said softly, then thought to add, "Thank you for asking. For being brave enough to ask and really mean it, I suppose."

Bruce didn't reply, only nodded without looking at her. His hands were still in fists, but his breath had calmed back down. Maybe she should have touched his arm or asked if he was okay, but all that seemed wrong.

She turned back to look at him one more time before going inside to where the guest rooms were. He hadn't moved.

The best thing was to just leave the sorrow hanging in the night air and pray the morning dawned a little more brightly.

Chapter Nine

Crying women usually made Bruce uncomfortable. In this case, however, Isabel's tears made him grin with satisfaction.

"They're so beautiful," she said between sniffs. They sat together at one of the dining room tables after church on Sunday, looking through the best of the shots he'd taken at the nature center.

"I'm so glad you like them. Olivia's a natural," he teased, touching the baby girl's tiny bare toes. The photos had turned out wonderfully. It was one of those successes Bruce could only put half down to his own talent. Clearly—to him, at least, and he hoped to Isabel—God had stepped in and worked His wonders.

Isabel stared again at the shot that had been Bruce's favorite as well. "I was afraid I wouldn't be able to like them. Being only the two of us, you know. Like I'd look at them and only see how William was missing."

The photo was a close-up of Isabel leaning down to Olivia, their two faces framed in a glow of sunshine pouring down through bright green leaves. Olivia's small fingers were reaching up to her mother, touching her cheek. The whole thing just radiated love and happiness. It had been a long time since Bruce had felt this proud of a shot—not because of the skill or daring needed to capture it but because of what it meant to the young mother.

"He's not missing. You just can't see him." That sounded sort of silly, like something a poet might say. He tried to laugh to lighten the mushy statement but found he couldn't.

Isabel looked up at him, gratitude in her eyes. "That's it. Exactly." Her voice wobbled again. "Daddy's there, isn't he?" she cooed to the child.

If each of the photos he took while here at Camp True North Springs had half the impact of this one, it would be astounding. "I know these were for you—and they are—but do you think we could use this one for the book? I think it might turn out to be my favorite."

Isabel thought for a moment. "Yes, of course. This place has meant a lot to me already. It'd be nice to know we were able to give something back." She grabbed Bruce's arm with her free hand. "Thank you. Really."

"It was my pleasure," Bruce said, meaning it. He flipped his tablet closed. "I'll have these and any other shots I get all on a drive for you at the end of the session. You can get prints made, or Christmas cards, or anything you like."

She gathered Olivia close, snuggling her in that precious, adorable way only mothers can do. There was so much love there. They must have been such a happy family. *Let them find happiness again, would you, Lord?* he prayed. *These two have a lot of love to give.*

Isabel looked up at Bruce. "Why are you doing all this? Donating all the photos? Did you lose someone, too?"

Bruce never quite knew how to answer that. He'd lost a lot but not in the same way as these people. "Mason's a friend. And I think it was just time to take some happy photos for a while." That was true. And it was the reason he had first said yes to Mason's request. It had become painfully clear now that God had brought him to Camp True North Springs for a deeper reckoning.

Part of that reckoning was due to happen with Jack in just a few minutes. "If you ladies will excuse me, I've got another lesson." With that, he stowed his camera and headed off toward the barn.

"Isn't the pond that way?" Isabel asked, pointing in the opposite direction.

"It is," he replied. "This is a different kind of lesson."

Why had she ever agreed to this?

Willa watched Jack shuffle his feet nervously as they waited for Bruce to arrive at the camp's massive barn. She understood what Bruce was trying to do, and in theory it sounded like a good idea. But now that it was happening, she felt a ridiculous panic grab her ribs.

Courage was overrated. Did a six-year-old need courage? Wasn't that what mothers were for—the whole *mama bear protecting her cubs* thing?

"You don't have to go with Mr. Bruce, honey. The whole point of us being here is that we don't have to do anything we don't want to."

Jack nodded. "I know. I wanna. And I don't. What's he gonna do?"

Bruce had asked her over coffee after the church service that morning what she felt Jack's fears were other than water. He said he was looking for something small, like her experience with the spider—although that hadn't felt small at all.

"Heights. He won't go up on the tall slide at school anymore," she'd replied.

Bruce had nodded, remembering. "I remember. You said he was more afraid of heights now."

She'd never thought of it that way, but Jack's insistence on taking the bottom bunk of the beds suddenly made sense. She'd truly thought the boys would fight over the chance to have the top berth.

After a moment's thought, Bruce had said he'd meet them back at camp after lunch, and he'd asked her to bring Jack to the big barn—the one that truly still served as a barn. Looking up now at the size of the barn, how it seemed to loom up to the skies next to Jack's tiny frame, Willa wasn't so sure.

Bruce walked up with his usual backpack, but he was also holding a large coil of rope and what looked like a pint-size version of the harness he was wearing.

"Is that what I think it is?" she nearly squeaked out. It looked too much like the one at the rock climbing gym where the twins had been invited to a birthday party back in Florida. Joe had leaped at the chance to go scurrying up the small man-made "cliff"; Jack had backed away as if the thing would eat him alive. It had turned out to be a stressful afternoon for everyone involved.

Bruce dropped the coil of rope onto the ground. "Relax, I'm not taking him scaling up the side of the barn."

Willa tried not to be embarrassed by the relieved sighs that escaped from her and Jack both.

"This is for you to feel extra safe while we go up the ladder that leads to the loft." Bruce pointed to a window just below the peak of the barn's roof. Anyone else would say it was just the second story. Willa watched her son swallow hard. "You and I will be able to take some amazing pictures up there. You're going to get to use my fancy camera. Would you like that?"

Jack's gaze bounced from the camera to the window and back again. "Can we use it down here?"

Bruce hunched down eye to eye with Jack. "We can. But the view is very cool, and you'll be very safe with me. We'll be linked together like real mountain climbers. And it's just a ladder, not a mountain. Are you brave enough to try?"

No, he's not, Willa whimpered in the silence of her thoughts.

"Dunno," Jack said, touching the camera as Bruce held it out and then craning his neck up to see the window.

I'm not, either. Which seemed embarrassingly silly. A barn loft was not Mount Everest.

And a tarantula was just a spider, right?

"It's up to you, buddy. But I think you can do it."

When he'd asked her permission for this little adventure—which didn't feel so little at the moment— Bruce had asked her to do her best to let Jack decide. She understood the logic in that. Children were resilient. Jack might indeed be braver than she was giving him credit for. And on her better days, Willa could admit she might have become a tad overprotective since

Rick's death. Still, time dragged at a glacial speed while Jack scrunched up his face, considering his options. She found it so hard not to answer for her son.

Finally, Jack straightened up and declared, "Okay. But I want the thing you got."

"Absolutely." Willa tried to let the warm smile Bruce gave both her and Jack fill her with a glimmer of confidence. Jack did need a win, a reason to feel proud of himself, and she'd run out of ways to give that to him. It was a stretch to think of Bruce Lawrence as a gift to her son, but perhaps it was true.

Bruce fitted Jack into the small harness with care and patience. He double-checked everything, asking Jack repeatedly if things felt okay. He surprised her by holding out the ropes and metal loop things—he called them *carabiners*—to her. "You should do the honors. Hook this part to Jack and this part to me. I want you to feel how secure they are."

The simple task felt enormous, as if Willa were somehow connecting Jack with this man in more ways than hardware. It felt both dangerous and necessary. As she clicked the carabiners to their places on each of them, Willa couldn't help feeling this was an essential leap of faith for all of them.

When Bruce shouldered the backpack with the camera and turned toward the barn, Willa sucked in a breath. When—as casual as can be—Bruce extended a hand down to Jack, and her son took it with a grin, that breath left in a gasp. Fear? Gratitude? Everything in between?

She was certainly grateful when Dana appeared beside her, watching the pair with a smile. "I heard about this. I think it's a great idea, if that helps. We seem to work the oddest little wonders here at camp, don't you think?" When Willa couldn't push a reply past the tightness in her throat, Dana asked, "You okay?"

"No," came the squeak of a reply. "But I'm trying."

Dana wrapped an arm around Willa as the climbers disappeared within the barn's massive doors. "Jack's not the only one being brave."

Willa yearned to dash into the barn and supervise the climb up the ladder to the small loft. Jack was only six. Still, Bruce had promised her he would stop and turn back if Jack asked at any point, and she believed he would. Which meant Jack had chosen to keep going. "It's a good thing he's doing," she said, half to Dana, half to herself.

"It is."

"He'll be okay," she reassured herself.

Dana looked at her with understanding in her eyes. "I absolutely believe he will. In fact, I believe he'll be a little bit better for the victory."

Willa kept her eyes glued to the large window on the second floor of the barn until, at last, Bruce appeared. He waved and gave her a thumbs-up. Then he turned away. She could easily imagine Jack hanging back, keeping a cautious distance from the window. She knew Bruce was coaxing him, but she believed the man would not lure Jack beyond his own capabilities.

When Jack's very nervous face appeared in the window, Willa knew in her heart her son had chosen this for himself. And yes, *victory* was the right word for it. Tears crept down her face as she waved wildly at Jack.

Dana gave up the loud cheer Willa's own tight throat couldn't manage.

Dana stayed with her the whole time she watched Bruce and Jack at the window. Bruce looped the strap around Jack's neck and helped Jack hold the big camera while they seemed to talk about which pictures to take. Even though she couldn't hear it, their conversation became less tense and more excited as Jack took shot after shot.

As she stood there, it struck her that Jack was making friends with the camera she'd declared her enemy. There was something deep and profound about that. Something she had to admit might pull them all toward healing.

Willa startled when Dana's cell phone went off with a text message, and she saw Bruce mime putting a phone to his ear. Catching the signal, Dana pulled out her phone. Dana's face was unreadable as she showed the text message to Willa. Jack wants to take a picture of you.

Willa let out a desperate gasp of a prayer. *Oh, Lord.* Could she really say yes to that? Even to her own son?

Willa thought of Jack's straight back and raised chin as he'd accepted the challenge from Bruce. The man was right—courage did come in all shapes and sizes.

She pulled in a breath as wide as the blue sky above them, looked up to the window and gave a nod. "Yes."

Chapter Ten

"And there's one of the mountain. And there's one of where the ducks live. And that's where we sleep. And some big clouds."

Bruce couldn't hide his grin as Jack wandered around the lunch table the next day, showing off his pictures. Bruce had loaded all the shots onto Jack's tablet—yes, kindergarten kids had such electronics these days—and the boy hadn't ceased displaying his photographs to anyone who would look.

"I think I just recruited my competition," Bruce teased Willa.

"Don't say that!" she shot back. "I couldn't handle Jack doing what you do. Ever."

"Just the photograph part, Willa. Not the other stuff." He looked at the boy with no small amount of pride. "I first caught the bug when I was not much older than him."

It was a pleasure to view Willa watching her son. His instincts had been right: the boys were hungry for a sense of accomplishment in their young lives. She was, too. Could she recognize that? Did she feel the change he so clearly saw in her since she'd let Jack face his fear? After all, she was facing up to her own desperation to keep them safe as she let Jack and Joe spread their wings.

He admired her for that. He admired her for a lot of things.

"I didn't expect Jack to ask you what he did," he admitted. "I'm sorry I put you on the spot like that yesterday."

Willa slanted him a glance. "Are you sure you didn't put him up to it? He's the only person on Earth I would let take my photo. You know that."

She was almost teasing, and he rather liked that, but Bruce could also see the wary pain in her eyes. The past few days had pushed her to her limits.

"I had no idea he'd do that," he assured her. "I promise you. And I almost told him no before I asked, but something stopped me. I think Jack knew, on some level, that he was the only person you'd let do it." Was it even fair to attribute such insight to someone under four feet tall? Bruce could only shake his head. "I don't know how else to explain it, but he knew what he was asking."

Willa gave a sigh. "That boy's been pushing my buttons since the day he was born. They both do. Only in such different ways. Amazing how different identical twins can be." She put her hand to her forehead. "And they haven't even hit first grade. How am I ever going to survive those two as teenagers?"

She gave a small chuckle at that. It was the first time he'd ever heard her laugh. She'd been under such a cloud of fear and sadness. Bruce liked the thought that he'd played a small part in the brightening of her spirit here at Camp True North Springs.

Jack made a comical face while showing yet another person his photos, and Willa smiled. Bruce liked her smile. The one in Jack's photo was forced, nervous and nowhere near as genuine as the one she gave now. *I was terrified to see her here, Lord. Now I'm glad You gave me the chance.*

That seemed a very dangerous thing to admit to the Almighty. God surely knew the gaping truth he was omitting, the enormous secret he was keeping from her. The irony of that followed him like a shadow. He was too afraid to tell her, too afraid it would destroy the fragile victory he was giving them. What business did a man of his cowardice have claiming to offer bravery to these two boys? To Willa?

A man of honor would tell her the full, painful truth and walk away. It was as much as lying to her to let this go on without her knowing the role he'd played in her life. Still, watching Jack, seeing how Willa's face changed as *she* watched Jack, Bruce couldn't bring himself to pull away.

A tug on his hand pulled Bruce from his thoughts. He looked down to see Joe trying to get his attention. He and Champion had been perusing Chef Seb's daunting selection of cupcakes set out for dessert, and he had a chocolate one in the hand not yanking on Bruce's arm.

"Hi, Mr. Bruce."

"Hi, Joe. Got one of those cupcakes, I see."

"I want three." Joe pouted at his mother. "Mom said I could only have one."

"You gotta listen to your mom. Plus, that's a pretty big cupcake. I could probably only handle one myself, and I'm twice your size."

"Grown-ups get to have as many as they want," Joe bemoaned.

"Well, you'd think, but we pay the price for too many cupcakes in other ways." Bruce patted his waistline.

"Some of us pay the price for any cupcakes," Willa added. It was the closest thing to a joke he'd heard from the woman yet.

Joe took a bite, and with his mouth still full of cupcake, declared, "I think I'm gonna get in the water soon."

He'd seen it so many times before—courage was contagious. While he hadn't planned it to be a tactic, Bruce had wondered if Jack's achievements would spur his brother into the water.

"Joseph Scottson, what have I told you about talking with your mouth full?" Willa scolded.

"She calls me that when she's mad," Joe admitted, oblivious to the fact that he was compounding his crimes by still talking with his mouth full.

Willa gave a groan—whether for "going in the water" or the mouthful of chocolate frosting, Bruce couldn't be sure—until Bruce held up a hand. "For a declaration of going in the water, I'll allow it. Just this once."

Willa pointed at her son, who promptly made a show of chewing and then swallowing his massive bite of cake. "I'm gonna get in the water," he repeated. "Pretty soon. The whole way in."

Bruce could almost hear Willa gulp beside him. "Okay, then," he said, somehow thinking *Glad to hear it* didn't quite fit the circumstances, even though he *was* glad. He wanted a big win for Joe just like Jack had gained yesterday. Still, that was asking a lot of Willa. And she'd been stretched far enough as it was.

"Hey, Joe, will you go get me one of those? As big as yours?"

Joe grinned—a smile adorably smeared with chocolate frosting. "Sure."

When Joe was out of earshot, Bruce asked Willa, "Are you okay with this?"

Her response was a fragile look. "I can't exactly back out now, can I?" The unspoken *Can I trust you?* he saw in her eyes cut straight to his heart.

He couldn't back her into a corner on this. That wouldn't be fair, especially after how she'd held up so far. "I'll find another way if you can't." He owed her that much. He owed her more than he'd given if he was being honest.

She pressed her lips together, and he could feel her efforts to muster up the courage. "We'll give it a try."

Bruce knew better than to promise her Joe's success, but every inch of him wanted to do it anyway. If he was going to have to walk out of their lives at the end of this session, he wanted to gift them with all the healing he could. A dozen things to say to her came to mind, but he stayed silent.

At least until Joe returned, with a cupcake in each hand. He lowered his eyebrows at the boy. "Didn't your mother say only one?"

Joe grinned at his mom, smears of chocolate still on his chin. "The pink one's for you." With that he presented the pink one to Willa and the chocolate one to Bruce.

Basking in her delighted smile, Bruce dared to lean in and whisper, "Sometimes they push just the right buttons."

Willa stared at Bruce. He couldn't seriously be making this request—this one request he had to know was the most difficult of all. Who was this man always asking so much of her? What happened to the Camp True North Springs that was supposed to be about healing and respite? The one dedicated to her family's needs?

Because this is about your family's needs, even if you don't want to admit it, her conscience chimed in with an unwelcome ring of truth. *You can't heal if you don't move on, and you can't move on without facing the thing you don't want to face.*

It wasn't entirely a surprise. Some part of her had always known this day would come. In a world filled with selfies and videos and a camera seemingly in everyone's hand, she'd have to make peace with it at some point. The boys were heading into first grade in the fall, taking tiny steps of their own out into the world. *You can't resist forever,* she told herself. If not him, would it be someone with less compassion, less understanding? Try as she might, at some point, she'd have no choice but to let certain things back into her life no matter how fiercely she'd kept them at bay.

"Jack asked you to take our pictures." Bruce had already told her this, but she needed another confirmation. It seemed both the most impossible and most probable thing, given her son's fascination with Bruce's profession. A cruel irony. Or a perfect invitation—depending on how you looked at it.

"He did," Bruce replied. "I promise you, it was not my idea." His face took on an intriguing expression. "Although I admit, I've wanted to. You shouldn't be left out of this. You deserve a portrait. The shots I took of Isabel and Olivia made me more sure of that than ever."

She'd seen how anxious Isabel had been over the photo shoot. And she'd seen how healing it had been, how Isabel treasured the photos and how Bruce had handled taking them. She might never find someone who understood the monumental nature of this first family portrait without Rick the way Bruce did. And it was her own son who had asked.

But photographs? Could she really agree to photos? It struck Willa that she already had, hadn't she? Jack had taken pictures of her from the barn window. Still, what Bruce was asking was different. Even if they were taken with the very same camera, they had larger implications.

Willa ran her hand along the garden fence where they were talking while Carson, the maintenance man was helping the kids plant garden stakes they'd made in an earlier arts and crafts class.

"We can take it slow." Bruce's voice was soft, his eyes warm and kind. "Not today, just sometime before the session is over. We can start with one or two shots of the boys having fun. Jack already thinks of the camera as his friend. I remember thinking that way when I was younger, too. I was a shy kid—"

"You?" she stopped him. "Shy?"

Bruce smirked. "I grew out of it. But partially because I had this companion of a gizmo that saw the world the way I told it to and froze it in time. He has that same eye, Willa. Photography did so much for me. It'd be such a sad thing to let the past take away the possibility of it doing the same for him."

People who hadn't lost enormous, precious parts of their lives always said things like that. They never understood that the heavier a past was, the harder it was to lay it down. And yet every other family here had talked about how hard—and helpful—it was to gain a new "family portrait" from Bruce. Isabel had said it reminded her she was still in a family, even with the loss of her husband. *Could I come to the same place?* Willa wondered. *Do I owe it to myself and the twins to at least try?* Bruce and his compassion toward her and the boys surely made him a better choice than some unfamiliar school or studio photographer sure to come down the road. Yes, he was a journalist, but he'd come to be something so much more in her view. She didn't know what to do with that shift in how she saw him. Or his camera.

"I've been meaning to say something," Bruce began, shifting his weight. "I know it'll sound weird. Or ridiculous. But I think it needs saying. If that's okay."

She'd never seen him quite so uncomfortable. It was sweet, although she couldn't quite say why. "Okay."

"I want to say I'm sorry. On behalf of all the people who do what I do for a living—all the nosy, insensitive, clueless photojournalists out there. I'm sorry for what happened to you. Whatever lout took that tape of Rick's drowning and thought for even one second it was okay to broadcast, he ought to be... Well, I'd have a few words to say to him that couldn't be said in front of your boys. It was wrong. It hurt you when you were already devastated, and it was everything wrong about journalism. I just need to say I'm sorry it happened."

Of all the things she'd expected to hear from Bruce, it wasn't that. The shock and the sincerity of his words tore down another piece of the defenses she'd begun to lose in this place. His words somehow found the core of pain still festering in her heart and cut it open. Cut it loose. Opened it to the world to release and heal. The sensation was so sudden and so powerful she gripped the fence to stay upright while the world seemed to shift under her feet.

"Willa…" He said her name with a tenderness that nearly undid her.

Did he realize the power of his words? The acute need to hear them she hadn't even known until this moment? She couldn't even begin to speak a reply.

"If nobody's ever said they're sorry for it—and I sure hope someone has—then I wanted to make sure you heard it from me. I'm sorry you were treated that way. I'm sorry your pain was used. Exploited. You and the boys both. And you have my word, if I ever discover a way to hunt down that tape, I'll make sure it's destroyed."

His heartfelt words pulled up a flood of remembered emotion. Dread. The wildly exposed feeling of knowing hundreds—if not thousands—of people saw the worst moment in her life. The shock that felt more like feeding some hungry beast than any kind of mourning or commiseration. The media's morbid curiosity struck her as one of the world's worst evils.

And yet none of that applied to the man in front of her. The irrational thought *If only he'd been there* popped up without warning. Of course, that made no sense at all, and it was a fool's errand to think along those lines. It was the earnest compassion in his eyes, his protective nature, that tugged at her.

Bruce winced and put a hand to his chest. "Don't cry. I didn't mean to make you cry."

She hadn't even realized a tear had slipped down her cheek. "I...um..." How could she explain the cloud of emotions surrounding her at Bruce's request and his words?

"I'm sorry. I said all the wrong things."

"No," she managed to say, pulling in a deep breath and an indelicate sniff. "You said all the right things, actually."

"I can't be the first person who's apologized to you for that footage, can I?"

"No," she replied. "I got a very nice and carefully worded letter from the television station. The kind of apology that looked like six lawyers drafted it." She couldn't believe she was actually laughing at her own words. Laughing had felt like a foreign language these past few years.

When Bruce gave a small laugh and a stricken look, she added, "It's just that you're the first person who actually sounds like he means it."

He shook his head. "Well, that speaks volumes for my field, doesn't it?" He looked down at the ground for a moment. "A lot of it is pretty awful stuff. Guys develop an appetite for the worst of life. Kind of why I'm here, actually. It was time to shake that off before I took one of those shots you can never take back."

She understood him a bit now. The odd passion he

brought to what he was doing here, the extraordinary care she'd seen him take with each family. "Better to take shots people will treasure, huh?"

His face lit up at her understanding. His smile warmed her in a way that she'd not felt in a long time. It was nice to have someone who cared, someone looking to keep her safe.

She gave him a warm smile in return, basking in the unfamiliar but pleasant way it felt. "How about adding ours to the batch?"

Bruce's smile glowed even more. All that charisma packed into such a heroic package—did the man have any idea how attractive he was?

"It would be my honor."

Chapter Eleven

Bruce had photographed some of the most astonishing things in the world, but these felt like the most important. He seemed to know the consequences of this shoot down to his bones. The need to get this right drove so hard through him that he had to keep reminding himself to calm down and stay steady. Joe and Jack would take their cues from him, and Willa's spirit would depend on her sons. If that wasn't enough pressure, Bruce was pretty sure this would be his only chance—his only opportunity to capture the perfect shot to redeem a host of things for this family.

You've got this. No sweat, right? he told himself. *Less dangerous than an avalanche. Fewer threats than a minefield.*

Prettier than the Alps at sunrise, some unruly corner of his mind added before he could think better of it.

Willa Scottson was, in fact, quickly turning into one of the most beautiful women he had ever known. Not in the standard way a man of his short and casual relationships usually noticed. She had a deep and hard-won allure. He kept thinking of all the "gold refined in the fire" scriptures, which really wasn't like him. She barely spoke of any kind of faith, but he could see it buried under all the pain. He could see that in all the families, but it called to him especially in Willa. He yearned to be able to show it to her.

That was a tall order for an already crucial photo shoot. *Help me,* he pleaded to God. *Show me how I capture that on film. If there's any way I can restore even a bit of the hope she thinks she's lost, You know I want to do that.*

Knowing that standing around being photographed always resulted in stiff, studio-ish portraits, Bruce had found a small tree out behind the house. When he told the boys to climb it, they scrambled up like a pair of monkeys.

"Be careful, boys," Willa cautioned. Bruce had intentionally chosen a very low tree, but mothers always worry. In truth, Joe and Jack were barely four feet off the ground.

"Sit there," he coached the boys, pointing to a thick low branch, "and let your mom stand between you."

Willa settled some more once the boys were within reach. He snapped a few shots of the boys enjoying looking down on their mother and the lovely tilt of her head, as she looked up to each of her sons in turn. The filter of sunlight through the leaves caught the extraordinary green of all their eyes and sent flashes of gold through the boys' mops of red hair. By all accounts, it was a well-framed shot—the kind you'd put on a Christmas card. Nice, but today had to go far beyond *nice.*

"Joe, tell your mom a silly joke." Boys that age had to know loads of those, right?

Joe told a goofy joke about a turtle and some cheese, and all of them broke into giggles. Giggles became outright laughs, and when Jack made what he called "a turtle face," Willa threw her head back and laughed.

Bruce's heart glowed and his shutter whirred through a dozen shots.

"Hey, Jack—whisper the craziest thing you'd ever eat into your mom's ear." Bruce had stayed up late last night, concocting a dozen prompts to get the family interacting and forgetting about the camera.

Willa's eyes popped wide at whatever Jack had whispered, and she looked at her son in total surprise. Again, Bruce's shutter captured a half dozen shots of the moment. He found himself laughing as well. "What'd you tell her?" he asked.

Jack pressed his lips together and scrunched his face up tight before saying, "Not telling."

Bruce raised an eyebrow at Willa to see if she'd reveal whatever had shocked her. She shook her head playfully. "Guess I'm not telling, either."

"Lemme try!" Joe said.

There was just enough competition in his tone that Bruce asked Jack, "That okay with you?"

"Yep."

Joe thought for a moment, then whispered in his mother's ear. Willa's startled expression was priceless. "You're kidding!" she exclaimed.

When Joe shook his head, she looked between her sons for a moment, then turned her gaze to Bruce. He tried not to let the bright and bubbly spark in her eyes sink deep into his chest. "They both said the same thing!" she said.

"Now I gotta know," Bruce said, feeling bright and bubbly himself.

Some version of *Nope* or *Not telling* came from all three of them—followed by ripples of laughter. A surge of gratitude went through him. This was turning out exactly as he'd hoped.

He took them over to the hill, then let them sit and tumble a bit on the grass. He perched them on the low wall of the memorial garden and on the porch steps. They were all having fun. Bruce was sure he'd get dozens of great shots. His photographs had graced covers and won awards, but Bruce knew he'd always be proudest of these.

The gorgeous colors of the low afternoon sun called for one extra set of shots—if he could manage it. Carefully, he asked Willa, "Can I get a few of you? I've got some of each of the boys on their own. I think it would make a great set if we could add some of you. But only if you're okay with it." He was dying to capture her strength and beauty, to allow her to see the beauty that was currently making his breath hitch. But he'd never take a shot from her that she wasn't ready to give.

"C'mon, Mom," Joe said. "Let Mr. Bruce take pretty pictures of you."

Her agreement was tentative at first. As if she didn't deserve "pretty pictures," when Bruce couldn't think of a woman who deserved them more. "Sit on the porch rail," he suggested, "and look toward the sun."

The breeze tossed her hair, and Bruce felt a little bit of his heart slip from his grasp as he captured the

"One Minute" Survey
You get up to **FOUR** books <u>and</u> a Mystery Gift...

YOU pick your books –
WE pay for everything.
You get up to FOUR new books and a Mystery Gift…
absolutely FREE!
Total retail value: Over $20!

Dear Reader,

Your opinions are important to us. So if you'll participate in our fast and free "One Minute" Survey, YOU can pick up to four wonderful books that WE pay for when you try the Harlequin Reader Service!

As a leading publisher of women's fiction, we'd love to hear from you. That's why we promise to reward you for completing our survey.

IMPORTANT: Please complete the survey and return it. We'll send your Free Books and a Free Mystery Gift right away. And we pay for shipping and handling too!

We pay for EVERYTHING!

Try **Love Inspired® Romance Larger-Prin**t and get 2 books and fall in love with inspirational romances that take you on an uplifting journey of faith, forgiveness and hope.

Try **Love Inspired® Suspense Larger-Pri**nt and get 2 books where courage and optimism unite in stories of faith and love in the face of danger.

Or TRY BOTH!

Thank you again for participating in our "One Minute" Survey. It really takes just a minute (or less) to complete the survey… and your free books and gift will be well worth it!

If you continue with your subscription, you can look forward to curated monthly shipments of brand-new books from your selected series, always at a discount off the cover price! Plus you can cancel any time. So don't miss out, return your One Minute Survey today to get your Free books.

Pam Powers

"One Minute" Survey
GET YOUR FREE BOOKS AND A FREE GIFT!
✓ Complete this Survey ✓ Return this survey

1 Do you try to find time to read every day?
☐ YES   ☐ NO

2 Do you prefer books which reflect Christian values?
☐ YES   ☐ NO

3 Do you enjoy having books delivered to your home?
☐ YES   ☐ NO

4 Do you share your favorite books with friends?
☐ YES   ☐ NO

YES! I have completed the above "One Minute" Survey. Please send me my Free Books and a Free Mystery Gift (worth over $20 retail). I understand that I am under no obligation to buy anything, as explained on the back of this card.

☐ **Love Inspired® Romance Larger-Print**
122/322 CTI G2AK

☐ **Love Inspired® Suspense Larger-Print**
107/307 CTI G2AK

☐ **BOTH**
122/322 & 107/307
CTI G2AL

FIRST NAME | LAST NAME

ADDRESS

APT.# | CITY

STATE/PROV. | ZIP/POSTAL CODE

EMAIL ☐ Please check this box if you would like to receive newsletters and promotional emails from Harlequin Enterprises ULC and its affiliates. You can unsubscribe anytime.

Your Privacy—Your information is being collected by Harlequin Enterprises ULC, operating as Harlequin Reader Service. For a complete summary of the information we collect, how we use this information and to whom it is disclosed, please visit our privacy notice located at https://corporate.harlequin.com/privacy-notice. From time to time we may also exchange your personal information with reputable third parties. If you wish to opt out of this sharing of your personal information, please visit www.readerservice.com/consumerschoice or call 1-800-873-8635. Notice to California Residents—Under California law, you have specific rights to control and access your data. For more information on these rights and how to exercise them, visit https:// corporate.harlequin.com/california-privacy.

LI/LIS-1123-OM

shot. She was like an epic heroine, her strong jaw and graceful neck tilted toward the gold light of the afternoon. He must have sighed or grunted or something, because she flushed and looked down. He caught that, too. Could she really not know how beautiful she was? It called to him so clearly, even buried under the pain and fear as it was.

He paused, startled by his own emotions. Somehow, without his even noticing, the guilt and fear he felt around Willa and the boys had been replaced. Or perhaps just overpowered. The affection welling in him couldn't stand. Whatever he felt had no hope of going anywhere or doing any good, other than allowing him to give his talents. To let them leave here a bit more healed. It was the camp's mission, and he'd come here to support the camp. Bruce just hadn't counted on it turning out so painfully personal.

Jack bumped his knee to get his attention. "Can we see 'em?"

Bruce was knocked out of his stupor. "Sure. Let me go get my laptop out of Dana's office so I can download them off the camera and you can see them on the screen." He smiled at the boy's eager eyes. "They're great." He also needed a few minutes to get his composure back where it belonged. "How about you all go in and see what Chef Seb's got set out for snacks? We can all sit around one of the dining room tables and look at everything."

Willa instantly agreed. He had to have only imagined the awestruck look on her face when she ushered the boys into the big house; it couldn't be there for real. Still, the particular glow in those stunning green eyes stuck with him as he followed them, turning the other direction toward Dana's office instead of toward the dining room, where the boys and Willa were headed.

Dana looked up from her desk at his entrance. "What hit you?"

"Huh?"

"You look like you were struck by lightning. Did the photo shoot go that badly?"

"Not at all. Went great." *Far beyond my imagination,* he added silently. Far too far, if that was a thing. Based on the thudding in his chest, it was most definitely a thing. He busied himself, gathering the gear out of his backpack, even as he felt Dana's eyes on him.

"Bruce?" She gave the word a lot of weight. For having only been Charlie's stepmom a short while, the woman had clearly mastered the *Something's up, don't lie to me* tone his own mother could wield like a weapon.

"Yeah?" *Please don't ask more.* To his dismay, she nodded toward the guest chair in front of her desk. Bruce sank into the chair with the reluctant air of a kid being called into the principal's office—for what? Caring too much?

"It's okay to get invested in our families. It's the whole point, actually."

Bruce fumbled for a way to respond without giving all the painful details. As far as he knew, only Mason was aware of the history between him and the Scott-sons. And yet Mason probably told Dana everything. People in love did that. It made him uneasy that she might know, but people who truly cared told the truth to each other. *You tell the truth to the people you care about.* If he wasn't feeling jagged enough already, that struck home hard.

The closer he grew to Willa and the twins, the more Bruce felt like his soul bounced back and forth between needing to spend more time with them and barely hanging on until they left. In truth, things were tipping much farther toward the *more time* side of things. Pushing out a breath, he ran a hand through his hair. "But they leave." He practically groaned the words like a pouting child.

"They do," she replied gently. "Sometimes that's the hardest part. I get it. You've done amazing things for Willa and the boys. I agree with Mason that it's no coincidence you were here."

Bruce swallowed hard. "You…know?"

"All Mason told me was that there are reasons why their presence hasn't been easy for you. You look a bit shook up, if you don't mind my saying. You okay?"

Shook up? That was one way to describe it. "I don't know. I'm not okay, I suppose. I hadn't counted on… on…liking them so much." That seemed an absurd thing to say.

Her smile made him feel worse. Or better. He wasn't sure which. "Or them liking you so much, I expect. The twins have really taken to you." She paused for a moment before adding, "And Willa. If you'd have told me two weeks ago that you'd be snapping portraits of all of them—of her—well, I'm not sure I would have believed it."

"Me neither." So much about these past couple of weeks had taken him by surprise. As he drove home at the end of every day, the singular thought humming through him was almost always *I'm so glad I didn't leave that first day*. Gratitude for the things he'd accomplished continually warred with the pain of who they were and the reason they were at Camp True North Springs in the first place.

They'd lost someone they loved.

On his account.

That couldn't stay hidden for long. If life had taught him one thing, it was that the scales always balanced out.

Willa felt a lump grow in her throat as Bruce paged through the photographs on his laptop screen. Could something be such a horrible pleasure? Hurt so much and soothe so much at the same time?

She touched his hand to pause the images at the one of her, Jack and Joe laughing. All those giggles in the sunshine—it was hard to believe the people on the screen were her and the twins. Somewhere along the way, she'd come to believe that they couldn't be that happy again. "It's precious," she whispered before she even realized she'd said the words out loud.

"Makes me smile just looking at it." Bruce's voice held the tone of wonder currently in her own heart. "Grabbing a moment in time like that—it's the best part of what I do." He sat back in the chair where they gathered at one of the dining room tables. "I take pictures of things, but the really good ones are of people. Been a while since I got to take shots of happy things."

She looked at him. "Are we happy things? Some days it's hard to feel like it." Most days.

"Marshall says we're goofy," Joe said. "I like goofy."

Jack pointed at the image. "Look at your tongue."

Joe peered at the screen. "Yeah?"

"It's sticking out all goofy. Marshall's right—you're a goofball." Jack twisted his face up toward Willa. "I like this picture better than the one I did."

"Oh, no," Willa replied to her son. "I like your picture of me." It felt like a turning point of sorts, one she was deeply aware Bruce had made happen. Jack had been a different boy since conquering the ladder. Happier—stronger, maybe. More like who he'd been before.

Jack made a face. "You look happier in this one. You look kinda weird in mine."

Willa remembered the forced nature of her smile for that shot, the *look calm, look happy* she'd been shouting at herself while her heart hammered in her chest. Could a boy as young as Jack pick up on that?

Bruce saved her. "That shot you took is of your mom being brave. Like you were. Brave is always good, but sometimes it's a different kind of good than happy." He turned his gaze toward the photos on the laptop screen, and Willa watched something come over his features. She wasn't sure she was ready to admit how much she liked the warmth she saw there.

"You ever hear someone use the words *a brave face*?" he asked the twins.

"Suppose so," Joe said. "On TV, maybe."

"You got the brave-face shot, and I got the happy-face shot. Both are great."

Willa felt her face flush as if Bruce had paid her a compliment. Perhaps he had. *It's been so long that I've probably forgotten how to recognize one.*

Bruce gave her the quickest of looks before saying, "Want to see my favorite?"

The boys said, "Sure," but Willa's chest tightened at what the shot would be. Knowing his favorite felt personal. Lots of things about Bruce were feeling personal.

He flicked through the images to the last three shots, then pulled up the middle one of her looking toward the afternoon sun. "This one," Bruce said in a softer tone.

Joe squinted at the shot and then looked at Bruce. "We're not in that one."

Now it was Bruce who seemed to flush. "Well, then, I guess it's my second-favorite shot. Any favorite would have to have the two of you in it, wouldn't it?"

His backpedaling went over the twins' heads, but Willa caught the deeper meaning. It sank into her chest before she could stop it, settling warm and surprising in a part of her heart that had felt cold for a long time.

"That's a pretty picture of Mom," Jack declared, completely innocent of what it might imply. "It's okay if it's your favorite."

Bruce kept his eyes locked on Jack, and Willa could easily guess why. She couldn't bring herself to look at Bruce after seeing this photo. It was a tender, beautiful portrait. She hardly recognized the woman in the picture. That woman was bathed in light and looked strong—things she could barely remember feeling. How could Bruce capture what wasn't there?

The answer came to her with surprising clarity: he couldn't. Which meant it was there. She hadn't lost it forever like she'd feared.

A surge of gratitude rose in her heart. She was the woman in the photo. And now she had proof. She'd have this photo that showed her. If anyone had ever told her she would come to treasure a photograph after everything that had happened...

Willa reached out and touched the screen, almost startled to feel the cool, smooth glass and not the warmth radiating out of the image. "Thank you. I like it." She almost said *I love it*, but that felt too daring.

Her words drew Bruce's gaze up to her. "Do you?" He seemed so pleased. "I think it's my favorite thing I've taken this year."

"You should put it on our wall, Mom," Joe suggested. "And the one with us. You know, on the wall where all the other pictures are."

"And some of my duck pictures," Jack added.

The wall of photos in the den. She'd kept them in perfect order, like a shrine to the happy family they once were. She'd never take any of the photos away, but perhaps it was time to add some new ones. Isn't that what Isabel had said—that she finally felt ready to add photos of "now" to all the ones from "then"?

"I think I understand what you've been trying to do here," she said to Bruce. She'd fought him so hard at first—for most of the session, actually—that he deserved that admission from her. "I'm sorry I put up such a fuss."

He had a charming smile. "No need to apologize. Not for a second. No one should ever force a photo on anyone. And that's a pretty hefty statement coming from someone in my profession. I guess I understand what you've been trying to do here, too."

Joe slid off his chair, evidently tired of the emotional conversation. "I'm done now. Can I go get some more popcorn?"

"Sure," Willa said. With that, Jack slid off his chair as well, and the twins dashed to the other side of the dining hall, where a big bowl of popcorn, a scoop and a stack of small paper bags stood waiting to feed hungry campers.

The thought of being alone with Bruce after so much emotional upheaval made Willa slightly anxious.

"I'll make sure you have all of these digitally," he said, reaching for a factual tone. "And I can even arrange for a few prints, if you'd like them. Joe's right—they belong on your wall somewhere."

"Thank you," Willa managed, afraid to say more.

"I...well I have a child's camera back at my place. It's left over from a promotion my paper did a while back. If it's okay with you, I'd like to give it to Jack. I really did mean it when I said he's got an eye."

While it felt overly generous, Willa didn't think she should refuse. "I think he'd like that."

A warm, too-close pause hung between them until Joe barreled back to stand between them, popcorn in hand. "Hey, Mr. Bruce, I got an idea for your next favorite shot."

Bruce turned to Joe, as seemingly glad for the break in the potent mood as she was. "What's that, buddy?"

"Me. All the way in the water. With my brave face on. At tomorrow's lesson."

Bruce looked at Willa, one eyebrow raised in a silent *You okay with that?* question.

She found herself nodding despite the knot in her gut. "One more for our wall, I guess."

Chapter Twelve

It's just a pond, Willa told herself the next day as she positioned chairs on the grass in front of the big house. She'd intentionally moved chairs for her and Jack closer to the water's edge than last time. They were still quite a ways from shore, but it didn't feel like it at all. *Remember the woman from the photo? That's you.* Jack had had his "brave face" victory; now it was time for Joe to have his.

Funny how today the barn ladder and loft seemed so much safer than a few inches of water.

Carol Owens set a chair down on the other side of Willa. "I thought I'd come offer some moral support."

"Thanks." Willa watched as Carol's son, Marshall, jogged down to the pond as if it were no big thing. It was no big thing for lots of people—would it ever be so for her? For the twins? It felt so petty and so insurmountable at the same time.

"I get it, you know," Carol said, watching her son playfully snap his towel at Champion as they moved onto the dock. The two mothers had fallen into a long conversation about the trials of raising boys the other night, and Willa had dared to admit her worries. She'd found Carol to be warm and friendly, not judging her fears the way some of the other mothers in Fort Lauderdale had. Everyone here understood how a tragedy could throw your fears out of whack, how one big disaster made you anxious that another could not be far behind.

"Don't you wish you were one of those calm moms who seem to take everything in stride?" Carol asked with a knowing smile. "The ones whose lives look perfect while they sip their coffee drinks in their yoga clothes? Middle school is full of 'em."

Willa had to laugh at the all-too-accurate stereotype. "So is kindergarten. Sometimes I think they look at me like I've wrecked the bell curve for motherhood for them. As if our existence is an unwelcome reminder that terrible things do happen." She grimaced at the other mom, ashamed of the judgmental words she'd blurted out. "That sounds awful, doesn't it?"

Carol sat back in her chair. "Maybe somewhere else. Here, I expect all of us get exactly what you mean. I love how Charlie explains it."

Mason's son, Charlie, struck Willa as an extraordinary child—one who'd come through a tragedy with a healing she hoped Jack and Joe could one day achieve. It made her eager to hear Charlie's take on this. "How does he explain it?"

"He calls it 'the squigglies.'"

Willa laughed at the term. "The *what*? Why?"

"That feeling you get when you know what's happened to you makes other people uncomfortable. We all know it. The conversations that stop when you enter a room, the low whispers they think we don't hear, that awkward moment when they try to think of something to say but end up saying something that only makes it worse…"

Willa put her hand on Carol's, relieved at how accurately the woman had put her own feelings to words. So it *did* happen to other people; it wasn't just her. "I do know that," she agreed.

"Charlie started calling them the squigglies when he was younger." Carol smirked. "Sounds right to me."

"Me too." After a second, Willa added, more quietly, "Only it's my stomach feeling something a bit stronger than the squigglies right now at the thought of Joe going in." *Or going under,* she added in her mind, feeling as if the cold water was rushing up over her soul. She felt she wouldn't be able to watch Joe's head go under the surface—even if on purpose—without yelling out. Or passing out. Where was all that courage Bruce kept telling her she had? Why couldn't she make herself feel more like the woman from the photo?

"You said he knows *how*, he just *won't*. Not since…" Carol raised an eyebrow.

"Neither of them," Willa replied. "None of us, actually."

"Like I said, I get it. I don't know what I'm going to do when Marshall gets old enough to drive. I've got half a dozen years to work up the nerve, but I think I'll need thirty. Teens in cars still feels like weapons to me. The boy who hit my Anna was nineteen. Wasn't even legal to have the drinks in him when he veered into the oncoming lane and took my girl from me." She shook her head. "No, sir, moms like us have big mountains to climb to send our babies back out into the world."

Willa was glad for the kindred spirit. She'd come here sure that she was so different from the other moms—so much more broken—only to learn how similar they all were. "It wasn't even my idea to come here. Our church gave us the trip and the session fee."

"Well, that was a lovely thing to do."

"I didn't see it that way at first," Willa admitted. "I only said yes because I thought Arizona would be the farthest place I could get from water." She sighed. "And here I am, trying to stay calm while I'm staring at a pond. *And* a swimming instructor."

Carol chuckled. "Who was it who said, 'If you want to make God laugh, tell Him your plans'?"

She'd heard the saying. "I don't know, but whoever it was, they got it right."

Carol settled back in her chair. Willa envied the woman's relaxation—every one of her nerves was still on high alert. "Well, at least he's nice to look at," Carol remarked with a teasing tone. "The man, I mean—although I suppose to the rest of us, the pond is pretty, too. I always fell for the book-smart type like my Arnie, but I suppose that rugged-handsome type appeals, too." She raised an eyebrow at Willa. "Bruce sure has taken a shine to your boys."

"I know I should be grateful," Willa confessed with a wince.

"But you're not?"

"I am, sort of." She wasn't sure she could explain the jumble of her feelings, but she wanted to try. "I know Jack going up on that ladder Sunday was because of

Bruce's encouragement. My head knows that's a good thing. But the rest of me isn't ready for this. It feels like too much, too soon." She dared to cast her gaze out to the calm circle of water in front of her. "That pretty pond just looks like a great big dark mouth waiting to swallow my son." She tried to find an open mind, to look at the pond with a hopeful perspective. It wouldn't come. She gave Carol a wilted look. "Do you think it will ever stop being so hard?"

"I sure hope so, but ask me again when Marshall gets his learner's permit." Carol tsked and shook her head. "Maybe we just learn to trust in the fact that they're braver than us." She gestured out toward the pond, where the three boys—Marshall, Champion and Joe—were joking around with each other at the water's edge. "You didn't think that'd be possible when you first got here, did you?"

"No."

"But you're here—and a good sight closer to the water yourself. I saw that iron grip you were giving the porch rail that first time. Maybe it only gets easier in tiny bits like this. Tiny bits that aren't really tiny at all, huh?"

"Maybe." A few days ago, "joking around at the water's edge" would have felt impossible. Now it was scary, but Willa tried to take solace in the fact that she was able to watch without going into a complete panic. After all, Bruce was right there. He'd been right there for Jack, and that had made a victory possible for her son. That was important. Essential, even. She was going to have to master this somehow, someday. If she could look at this trip as a gift—yes, a challenging one, but a gift nonetheless—then maybe it was possible. If she could do it for Jack, then she owed the same to Joe.

The boys were laughing. They were playing as if the pond was not a giant Joe-eating monster. Joe even surprised her by following Marshall and Champion when they dashed back out onto the dock. Willa gripped the chair's arms and told herself it was okay. Bruce was right there, Joe was having fun and it would be okay.

"No running on the dock!" Bruce called out. "Come on back over here. Time to get started."

The boys bumbled around each other to turn around and head back toward Bruce. Willa could barely believe Joe was laughing as he did so. Was this the same Joe who'd been so frightened the other day? Was such a big change possible for such a little boy?

Willa was just telling herself to smile and wave when Joe wobbled, gave a yelp, and tumbled headfirst off one edge of the dock and into the water.

It happened all at once: Willa's horrified scream, Joe's startled yelp of panic, the sudden stop of the laughter the boys had been sharing, and the quiet but earth-shattering splash of Joe hitting the water. Bruce saw it all at the same moment every inch of his body sprang into action, instinct and training meshing with a surge of guilt and regret that felt like a volcano—simmering for years and now erupting.

"Joe!" Willa screamed as she catapulted herself out of the chair where she'd been sitting with Jack and Carol Owens. "Joe!" she called out again as she sprinted toward the water. Just before his own body hit the shallows, Bruce caught sight of Willa's and Jack's faces. Their eyes were wide with utter terror.

Fueled by their expressions, Bruce crossed the distance between him and Joe in three strides, then wrapped his arms around the boy in seconds as he flailed in the water beside the dock. "You're okay. I've got you," he called out, with a confidence he came nowhere near feeling. "Steady, Joe. Steady. You're okay."

It was shallow enough that Bruce could easily stand in the water, but that wasn't true for Joe. Some deep instinct overrode Bruce's first impulse to just yank the boy from the pond. He was frightened but not hurt. He looked around wildly but wasn't crying. He had to try to give the boy a sense of survival, some hint that while scary, that fall hadn't done him any harm. "You know how to swim," he said in a steady tone. "You're okay, Joe. Look at me."

The boy's panicked squirming died down a little.

"That's it. Eyes on me. Take a deep breath. It's just water. It didn't hurt you. You're okay."

Joe coughed, and Bruce heard Willa's cries from behind him. Even turned away from her as he was, he could picture her struggling at the edge of the pond, needing to dive in after her son and being unable to do so. Had he not been there, Bruce had no doubt Willa would have hurled herself into the pond to reach Joe. Mothers did that. Willa would brave any danger for the sake of her boys.

Still, he *was* here. The key truth, if he could just get everyone to hang on to it, was that Joe was not in danger. Yes, he'd fallen into the water, and the sputtered coughing told Bruce he'd been rightly scared. But even in the midst of all the drama, Bruce's deeper instincts told him that what he did next—what Joe did next— might shape the boy's relationship with water for the rest of his life. He had to try to give Joe a healthy way through this.

He kept repeating the same things in a calm tone: "Look at me, Joe. You're okay. You're in the water, and that's scary, but you're okay."

He felt the boy's iron grip on his arms loosen up the slightest bit. Joe looked at Bruce, struggling to grasp what he was hearing.

"We're so sorry, Joe," came Marshall's worried voice as he jumped off the dock and into the water to stand beside Bruce and Joe. "But you're okay. See that? You're okay." Marshall put a hand on Joe's still-shaking shoulder. "You just slipped, but you came right back up again."

Their assurances weren't working. "I wanna get out," Joe whimpered. The water was still his enemy. Bruce felt his chest fold in on itself with the failure of it all. The progress, the tiny joy of his feet splashing at the shore with him a week ago—all wiped out within a matter of seconds.

"You got it," Bruce said, gathering the boy up in his arms. He forced a *no big deal* tone into his voice despite what he was feeling. He'd hoped to get Joe calmer before he got out of the water, for Joe to take away a steadier memory than what he had right now, but that wasn't going to happen.

"Joe, honey, you're okay," came Willa's voice.

As Bruce turned with Joe still tightly held in his arms, Bruce saw a sight he knew would never leave him: Willa, shaken to her core, standing ankle-deep in the pond, with Jack beside her. One hand clung to Jack while the other reached out to Joe.

Like every small child, Joe had been holding his tears at bay until he saw his mom. At the sight of her and her expression, Joe dissolved into tears. The second they were close enough, he scrambled out of Bruce's grip to lunge at his mother so hard he sent Willa and Jack tumbling to sit in the shallow water.

Bruce stood there, dripping in the shallows, watching Joe burrow into his mother's shoulder. He saw Willa's arms clamp fiercely around her son like a set of maternal armor. Even Jack, still locked to his mother's side, wrapped one small arm around Willa while the other settled on his brother's back.

He'd failed them. Again. Anguish nearly knocked him over, made him want to sink into the grass and mud and hide. Still, he made himself stand there and take it, stand knee-deep in the pond until she managed to look up at him.

It wasn't hatred he saw in her eyes. It wasn't disappointment or gratitude that her son was safe. It was betrayal. She'd trusted him, trusted his promise that he'd keep Jack and Joe safe while they faced their fears, and he'd failed her. He tried to say *I'm sorry*, but the words couldn't climb past the choking in his throat. He wanted to keep telling Joe he was okay, to let Willa hear him say it, but things were far from okay.

Carol called Marshall and Champion off the dock, but Bruce barely noticed. The world pared down to the three of them and an oddly frozen sense of time. People moved around him; he dimly registered them saying things, but Bruce couldn't move.

Stopped as the world was, a strange and piercing thought came to him: they were in the water. Jack, Joe and Willa were all in the water. The thing he'd strived to achieve—the thing he'd prayed for—had happened.

But it had ruined everything.

As if she'd somehow heard his thoughts, Willa struggled to scoot herself and the boys the few feet to the shore without releasing them from her tight embrace. They were in only inches of water, but Bruce could see Willa's whole body react to being back on land. He knew the minute her legs would carry her, she'd dash back up the grass and probably never set foot anywhere near the pond again. The boys as well.

He'd made everything worse. He'd taken his eyes off Joe for one minute, wrongly thinking he was okay on the dock with Marshall and Champion. He'd even enjoyed the sound of Joe's laughter, thinking it heralded a close victory for the boy.

If a man could drown in defeat, this must be what it felt like.

"Let's go." Willa's voice was bitter and tearful.

The boys nodded, and Bruce watched the family scramble to their feet. Without a single look back, without even stopping for the towel and shirt Joe had left on the shore, they walked to the barn and disappeared inside.

Last night, Bruce had decided he might actually tell Willa what had happened, how he had failed to come to Rick's aid. He planned to ask her forgiveness, to reach for something that might help to heal them both.

That would not—*could* not—happen now. There

would be no forgiveness, ever. Some things were un-forgivable, even with an ocean of God's grace.

The walk out of the few feet of water loomed a mile long. Bruce felt as if the best thing he could do was walk straight toward the camp's gate and keep walking.

Chapter Thirteen

Bruce didn't really know how long he'd been standing there, feeling as if he'd turned to cold stone despite the fierce Arizona heat. He was dimly aware that someone had walked up to him, but he hadn't turned to look.

"Won't help," came Carson Todd's voice beside him.

Bruce blinked, trying to push his way out of the fog of despair wrapped around him, and managed to turn toward Carson. "Huh?"

"I know that look—like the world would be better off if you just walked out that gate and never came back. Trust me, it won't help. It'll just follow you."

"I failed him. I promised Willa he'd be safe, and I failed him." The word *failed* seemed to grow sharp edges that sliced at him.

"Maybe. Maybe not."

Bruce glowered at him. "How can you say that?"

"The ugly truth we all bump up against here is that you can't ever keep anyone safe. It's a promise that never holds. A lot of people go through life never realizing that, but every single person here knows it."

Bruce felt too wounded to appreciate the maintenance man's philosophy at the moment. "He fell in, Carson. I was supposed to make it safe for him, give him a victory over this, and he *fell in*."

"He did. He also got back out."

Bruce dared to say the thing lurking, dark and burning, in his chest: "His father didn't."

"And that's just it, right there. He got a good scare, one we all probably wish didn't happen, but Joe knows now you can fall in the water and be okay." Carson put a hand on Bruce's shoulder. "I heard what you said to him. I think it'll sink in. Not right now, of course, but it will. So if you ask me, you didn't fail the boy."

Bruce looked at the shut-tight door of the barn where Willa's rooms were. "I doubt Willa agrees with how you put that."

Carson shook his head. "Well, I expect she's a bit undone at the moment. And you may not get a picture-perfect happy ending on this one—but I wouldn't put it in the failure column just yet."

Bruce felt his legs finally give way underneath him, and he sank onto the sandy bank of the pond's edge. Today couldn't be anything but a failure. He'd started to believe that this time at Camp True North Springs could hold redemption for him, but he was wrong. It had torn him up to fail some unknown mother of two years ago, but it was far worse to fail Willa Scottson and her sons. Because he cared about them. He cared *for* them. He'd even started to entertain the impossible idea that he could be part of their lives after the camp session was over. It couldn't happen now. Who had he been kidding that it ever *could* happen?

"You ever heard anybody say 'It's not how you fall, it's how you get back up'?" Carson asked.

Bruce grumbled something close to "Yes."

"The thing about dumb sayings like that is, they're usually true. Only in this case, it's closer to 'It's not how you fall *in the water*, it's how you get back out of it.'"

Carson was just trying to help. He didn't deserve the dark look Bruce gave him.

"I've fallen into a lot of deep water in my day. Miles-deep stuff." Carson picked up a rock on the sand between them and tossed it far into the pond. "I say it's true. You got back out, and you made sure Joe did, too. We don't all get the clean, easy victories, Bruce. Some of us get the ugly, scrambled ones. But they work, too. So don't walk out of that gate."

Bruce narrowed his eyes at Carson. "I have to. I don't live here."

Carson gave a dark laugh. "Then make good and sure you walk back in tomorrow. Now's not the time to give up on Joe or Willa. Now's the time to hang in there and fight for that ugly win."

Bruce hauled himself to his feet, despite feeling like he was made of lead. As if he'd sink to the bottom of the pond if he dared put a foot in it now. "You should stick to fixing things. Pep talks aren't really your thing."

Carson put his hand to his chest. "Ouch, man. Cut me some slack here." He held out a hand. "I want your word you'll come back tomorrow, no matter how lousy you feel." He kept the hand extended until Bruce gave in and shook it. "We'll see to Willa and the boys tonight. It'll get sorted out."

Bruce didn't buy the confidence in Carson's tone. "And how do you know that?"

Carson picked up the shirt and towels still lying on the grass. "You know what happened to the last person I failed on a massive scale, don't you?"

This wasn't really the time for a long story, but Bruce replied anyway, "No, what?"

Carson grinned. "Earlier this year, I married her."

Willa asked Nelly and her mother to play with the boys while she pulled Dana aside at the campfire after dinner that evening. "Can we talk?"

"Of course," Dana answered. "I've been worried about you. How is Joe? How are all of you?"

Willa rubbed her hands together. "Joe's shaken up. We all are. I know it may seem like a small thing—"

Dana stopped her. "Don't feel you have to apologize. It's not a small thing at all. Everyone here understands that. Trauma doesn't play fair, and things can blindside us in ways other people don't understand."

Leading Dana a little farther away from the group, Willa said, "You all have been very nice, and I appreciate all you've done, but I think it's best that we head home this weekend. Can you help me arrange that?"

Dana's shoulders sank. "Of course, I'll do whatever you want—but are you sure? I want to encourage you to stay. Some of the most powerful things we do here at camp are coming up in this final week, and I'd hate for you to miss them."

She'd heard something of the sort from Bridget when she'd taken Joe into the nurse's office to make sure he was okay. "The little ceremony where they send remembrance flowers out into the pond?"

"Among other things, yes."

"I was dreading that, actually." Willa looked out over the landscape. Where was the dusty, dry desert she'd thought she was running to? Why did so much here have to do with water? "Honestly, I don't really know why we ended up here. It all seems like some very bad joke. Like God got us mixed up with some other family and sent us here by mistake."

Dana put a hand on Willa's arm. "You don't really believe that, do you?"

"I suppose not. But it still all feels wrong." Willa looked up at the evening sky. She'd marveled at the color many nights, but tonight it felt inky black and too large. "I don't know what it is we need, but this doesn't feel like it. We're better off going home before something else happens."

"Can I tell you something?" Dana asked.

"Sure."

"Do you know how many people have told me or Mason that they want to leave before the session is done? The things that happen here are hard. Lots of us want to run from the growth that seems to get asked of us here. I did. Seb did. Bridget did—and a bunch of other camp families who came before you. You're not alone in feeling this way."

Dana probably thought that would help, but it didn't. Willa still felt betrayed. Tricked into hoping something good would come out of their time here, only to discover it wasn't to be. Staying the next full week felt like it was simply inviting more pain.

"We tell them all the same thing," Dana went on. "Give it a bit more time. Give us until Monday. The flights are more expensive on the weekends, anyway. Please."

Willa didn't reply. She wanted to leave right now, but Dana was trying so hard to convince her to stay.

"I still believe God has something important in store for you here. Really, I do. And think about Jack. Good things have happened for him, haven't they?"

That's what hurt the most. Jack had gotten his victory, his moment of courage. Even she had known a moment of hope in agreeing to and seeing Bruce's photos. But Joe? He'd been let down. It didn't seem fair. "Not for Joe," Willa said, not bothering to tamp down the bitter edge to her words.

Dana gave Willa a long, direct look. "That's true. And that hurts. But if you leave, you take away any chance for him to get his good thing. That is your choice, and I'll respect it, but you need to know I've seen a lot of amazing things happen here because people were willing to give things one more try or a little more time. I've seen God work wonders against staggering odds. I have to believe that's true for Joe as well. For all of you."

Willa understood Dana's thinking but was too emotionally spent to embrace it. The urge to stomp off back to Florida, shouting, "I told you so!" burned in her chest. That was more like something Jack or Joe would do than the wise mother she was supposed to be.

"Please tell me you'll think about it," Dana urged.

"I don't know," was all Willa could reply.

"Have you spoken to Bruce?"

"What good could that do?" *I'm angry with him.*

He promised me Joe would be safe. Why would I talk to him now?

"He's broken up about what happened. I think it would be worse for everyone if we just left it at this, don't you?" Dana paused before asking, "Have you asked Joe about it? What does he say about what happened to him?"

Willa stared back at her sons roasting marshmallows over the fire. They didn't look wounded—certainly not as wounded as she felt. And Dana was right: it wasn't realistic to think she could pack them up this minute and call a cab to take them the three hours to the Phoenix airport. Had she walked up on the scene in front of her just now, without knowing what had happened earlier in the day, she might even say the boys looked happy. Joe had gone back to the room, cried a bit, fallen asleep and then woken up in a surprisingly decent mood. The rest of the day had felt…absurdly ordinary.

"Joe says he fell in the water and it was scary." She didn't want to admit the next part. "He also says Bruce told him that he was okay. That it was just water and that he could be scared but okay."

"That sounds good." Dana raised an eyebrow in encouragement. "A healthy way to look at it, don't you think?"

Willa knew it was *she* who clung to her own bitterness and anger—and it did not feel good to admit that at all. "In fact," Willa forced herself to admit, "Joe's exact words were, 'I didn't get to my brave face.'"

Dana gave a small laugh. "That does sound like something Bruce would teach them. But, Willa, do you hear his words? 'I didn't *get to* my brave face?' To me, that says he thinks his brave face is still out there waiting for him."

Willa had done her best to ignore the same thought. "It feels too hard." Her words were almost a whine. So very far from the woman in Bruce's sunny photo.

"We'll be here for you." Dana gave Willa's hand a reassuring squeeze. "Please stay. At least over the weekend. Give yourself time to talk to Bruce, or let the boys talk to him. God is up to something here—I know it."

"I sure don't."

"Well, we're fine with knowing it for you. Mason and I have faith to spare. You can borrow as much as you need."

Chapter Fourteen

Bruce stayed away from camp on Saturday, despite Mason's urging to come back. He needed time to think about how to respond, and everyone probably needed a day to calm down.

He quickly learned that staying away only made it worse. After a miserable Saturday, Bruce counted the hours until he knew the families would be back from service and drove through the camp gates Sunday afternoon.

Nervous, doubtful he could pull this off, he found Joe and Jack on the porch steps and walked up to the boys. Their eyes were a mix of things, as if neither boy knew how he felt—or ought to feel. *I get it, boys,* Bruce thought. *This is hard for all of us.* He shot up a quick, wordless prayer that God would give him the words to make things right with the boys…

…and with their mother. Willa's expression on the porch behind Joe and Jack was even more of a puzzle than her sons'.

Bruce hunched down on the porch steps and set down the bag he was carrying. "Hi, guys," he ventured.

"Hi," Jack and Joe said in unison.

"How are you feeling today, Joe?"

Joe looked down at the porch boards. "Okay."

Bruce sat fully down on the porch steps and motioned for the boys to sit as well. Willa sat in a chair a short distance behind them. He could feel her eyes watching him. There was plenty he wanted to say to her, but the boys were the most important at the moment. When Dana had called him and told him she'd barely talked Willa out of leaving over the weekend, he knew he had to come. There were things to be said. Things he would not miss the chance to say—especially if she followed through on leaving before the session was over.

"Friday was hard, huh?"

Joe nodded.

"For me, too. I didn't want that to happen, and I should have been more careful to make sure you didn't fall." Bruce fought the tightness in his throat. "Will you forgive me, Joe?" This family had come to mean so much to him. "You don't have to say right now, but I want you to know I'm really sorry, and I hope you will forgive me someday."

Joe raised his eyes to meet Bruce's gaze. "S'okay. You were right—I didn't get hurt or anything. Just scared."

The boy's quick forgiveness sank into Bruce's chest and cut loose the iron bands that had been crushing his breath for the past two days. "Thanks, Joe. That means a lot. And I'm really glad you're fine." He reached into his bag. "I want to give you something. Is that okay?"

"Yeah."

Bruce pulled out two decorated metal disks. "This is a pair of challenge coins. I got them from a friend of mine in the Special Forces. A soldier. It's sort of a thing they do. I asked him to give me these two just for you." He put one in Joe's hand; the large coin practically filled the boy's palm. "They're both the same. This side here? That says 'Fear.' Turn it over."

Joe flipped the coin to peer at the other side. "This side says 'Courage.' It's supposed to remind you that courage is always on the other side of your fear."

"My brave face," Joe said.

"That's right. When you get to your brave face about the water, you can put that someplace special to remind you how you found your courage on the other side of your fear."

Joe scrunched up his face in a way that let Bruce know he might not have grasped the concept. But the look on Willa's face a few feet away let Bruce know the point had sunk home with her.

"Why are there two?" Jack asked.

"That's the best bit." This part wasn't classic challenge-coin culture, just something Bruce had made up while staring at the coins. He'd originally asked his military buddy for the two so that he'd have one for each boy, but a far better idea had come to him yesterday. "There's two because you get to throw one away."

"Huh?"

"When you do get into the water and find your brave face, I want you to take this one coin and toss it in. Let it sink to the bottom of wherever you are. You get to leave your fear behind. It'll be gone, just like the coin. But the courage, you get to keep that. Forever. So that's why you have the second coin—to keep."

Bruce took Joe's smaller hand in his and wrapped

the boy's fingers around the coin. The moment felt important. Redemptive. If he couldn't get Joe all the way to his courage here at Camp True North Springs, he could help Joe find it one day in the future.

"What do you think?" he couldn't help but ask.

"It's neat," Joe said. He held up a coin in each hand. "I like 'em."

"I'm glad." He turned to Jack. "I have something for you, too."

"More coins?" Jack asked.

"No, something different." He pulled a box from his bag. "This is a camera for somebody your age. It's not as fancy as mine, but it's perfect for you to start taking pictures. I asked your mom earlier if I could give this to you, and she said it was okay."

The sight of Jack's wide eyes as he took the box set a glow under Bruce's ribs. "This is mine?"

"It is now. It'll take pictures your mom can send to her tablet or get printed. That wall in your house should have a few of your photos up on it, right?"

Jack opened the box to pull out the rugged plastic camera and hold it with awe. "Wow."

"But I want you to make me an important promise."

"What's that?"

"Don't ever take a picture of someone without their permission. Animals and stuff from nature or your toys is okay, but people have to be asked first. Especially your mom. Got it?"

Jack nodded. "Got it."

Bruce gave Jack's hand a serious shake. "You're a photographer now. I expect great things from you."

"'Cause I already got my brave face?"

Bruce laughed. "For that and a lot of other reasons."

At that moment, gifts duly given, Bruce allowed himself to look up at Willa. Her eyes glistened. He'd done what he'd come to do. Well, almost. He had one important bargain he hoped to strike with Willa—if she'd give him the chance.

Bruce rose to his feet. "Okay if I talk to your mom for a minute?"

Jack said, "Sure."

But Joe surprised Bruce by piping up, "I gotta ask you something first."

The way the young boy's chin stuck out in determination tugged at Bruce. He was going to miss their daily presence in his life. And not just the boys' but Willa's. "Ask away, buddy."

Joe clutched a coin tightly in each hand. "Can I still get my brave face?"

Bruce felt the question hit him like a wave. That was the last thing he'd expected Joe to ask. Was Willa ready for that? Was *he* ready for that? Whether either of them were ready, it was obvious that Joe was. "Here at camp?" Bruce tried not to sound astonished.

"Yeah." Joe shrugged. A child's resilience was the most amazing wonder. "I'm okay. And all I did was get wet. I wanna swim tomorrow. I wanna toss the coin in the pond."

Was it possible for a person's heart to sink and rise at the same time?

Willa felt her emotions go in ten different directions at Joe's request. Some part of her knew he'd not been as undone by his fall into the water as she had. Her pulse had stopped when Joe's head went under the water, a remembered utter terror surging through her. Her rush to the shore had felt like wading through quicksand, her feet trapped in cement the minute they hit even the smallest bit of water. *I'm not sure I can do that again.*

Bruce's expression as he walked toward her was as complicated as her own feelings. He understood everything involved in Joe's simple request—it wasn't simple at all. Friday night's urge to run still thrummed in her veins. Why couldn't she just escape down the mountainside and leave all this hard risk and growth behind? Why was life asking all these hard things from her when she was supposed to be here to heal?

Bruce spied someone over her shoulder. "Vanessa," he called out, "could you hang out with Joe and Jack for a minute while Willa and I talk something over?"

Joe, no fool even at six, pronounced, "I wanna try and swim again," to Vanessa, evidently hoping to gain an ally.

Vanessa's expression shifted from surprise to a knowing smirk. "Well, that does require a conversation, doesn't it?" She smiled at the boys. "Come on over here and join Champion and I while we take a crack at this puzzle." She raised an eyebrow at Willa. "Take all the time you need."

The minute they came down off the porch, sufficiently out of earshot, Willa pleaded, "I was looking into leaving tomorrow. Now what do I do?"

"I get it," Bruce surprised her by saying. "And you'd have every right to. But I was hoping you wouldn't. Now I'm *really* hoping you wouldn't."

She pushed away the hair the hot wind kept blowing

in her eyes. "I don't have another week of this in me.
Joe's just going to have to get his brave face some other
time." Even as the words left her mouth, they sounded
sour and selfish. She didn't want to take this experience
away from Joe, especially in light of Jack. And then
there were the gifts—Bruce's extraordinary, thought-
ful gifts that had brought tears to her eyes. They were
all good reasons to try to stay the few more days they
had left in the session. Except she was sure she had no
more trying left in her.

Bruce stopped walking under the tree where he'd
taken those first cheerful photos of her and the boys.
Did he do that on purpose, or was that just God pressing her to her limits?

"Willa…" There was anguish in how he said her
name. She offered no reply.

"Those were meant to be goodbye gifts. Things I
wanted to give the boys in case I never see them again
after today."

His sentiments just pulled at her heartstrings all the
more. "Thank you," she managed.

"I need to ask your forgiveness, too. I know what
Joe's fall into the water did to you. After you trusted
me to keep him safe. I'm so sorry."

Willa knew she ought to say something like *I forgive
you*, but she couldn't reach for that response just yet.

"I know this was a long shot of an ask before, but
given what Joe just said, I'm still going to ask it." He
put his hand on the big branch where Jack and Joe had
sat, as if it would somehow help to hold him upright.
"I know you want to run away from all this. I do, too.
After Joe fell, I wanted to crawl away. I stayed away

yesterday, thinking I ought to never come back. I even called my old assignment editor and asked for the most immediate, most far-away assignment he had."

Willa looked back at the porch, where her sons played with Champion. What did Bruce's next photo assignment have to do with her?

"I haven't even told Mason this yet, but I accepted an assignment. I leave on Tuesday to be imbedded in some troops in Poland. I won't be here for the rest of the week. Tomorrow will be my last day here."

"That sounds…dangerous," was all Willa could think of to say.

"No more than usual," Bruce offered with a calm she found disturbing. How did people do that sort of thing all the time?

"Willa," he said with enough intensity to draw her gaze. "I'll call him back and turn it down. I'll stay and see this through if you do."

"You're serious."

"I mean it. I know you want to walk away, and you have every reason to." He shifted his weight and flung one hand back toward the porch. "But can we take this chance away from him?"

I'm his mother. Of course I can, her weary brain snapped back silently.

"One more chance. That's all he needs." After the longest moment, Bruce added, "That's all I'm asking for. And although I may just blow up my professional credentials by going back on this assignment, I'll do it. I'm ready to risk that for your son. For both of them. Because I'm pretty sure once Joe gets back in the water, Jack won't be far behind."

She knew that. Sometimes their competitive nature—even at this age—was a challenge. Maybe it would be nice to wield it for good. But two sons in the water? Her heart wilted just thinking of it.

"Willa, please." There it was again—the anguish in how he said her name. As if his life was somehow locked to hers in ways neither of them could escape. Maybe it was. Dana and Mason were right: it couldn't be coincidence that they'd landed here at Camp True North Springs together.

"I'll walk out of here right now and pack my bags if you say so. I'll find a way to make it okay for Joe to find his brave face with…with someone else. But I don't want to. I want to make this right. For them. And for you."

How had he come to care so much for two boys he'd only known for a little over two weeks? How had he been the one to show her the woman of courage she'd thought gone for good? If she refused, if she exercised her perfectly reasonable right to keep her boys safe, some part of her knew she'd regret it. She'd always wonder what would have happened if Joe found his brave face here, with Bruce.

"Okay." She felt like she ought to have choked the word out, but it just lifted out of her, light and stunningly easy.

Bruce's face lit up, and he grasped her hand. It was an impulsive thing, but the strength of his touch shot through her. He flushed, let go and shoved his hand behind his back as if he needed to corral it from straying toward hers again. She knew, in that moment, that he'd felt whatever it was she'd felt.

"Go find my son's brave face tomorrow," she said. Her words had the tone of a command, like some princess knighting a warrior to defend her empire. Less eloquently, the back of her mind silently added, *Don't make me regret this.*

"Thank you." She saw his eyes glisten a bit as he put the disobedient hand to his chest.

It's now or never, she thought. She had to give this knight every bit of armor she had for the quest before him. "Bruce?"

"Yes?"

"I…I forgive you."

He ran his hands down his face, squinting back a threat of tears. *What do you know? It* does *make you feel lighter to offer forgiveness.* Even if she didn't truly feel it, just saying the words did change the way she felt. It undid some of the knots and made her breaths come easier.

He tried to say something—twice—but choked on the surge of emotion she could see in his features. In the end, he just nodded, held her hand again for just a second and then walked toward the big house.

Bruce Lawrence was already a big man, but Willa was sure he held himself an inch or two taller as he walked away.

Please, Lord. She didn't even know what it was she was supposed to be asking for. So she just settled for saying *Please, Lord,* over and over.

Chapter Fifteen

Bruce wasn't sure when this had turned into a team effort. Every other child at the camp—except for baby Olivia, of course—was lined up at the water's edge Monday morning to cheer Joe on. That was either the most amazing show of community or a whole lot of peer pressure. Bruce wasn't sure which. *Be with me, with us,* Bruce prayed as he walked over to where Willa, Jack and Joe sat.

The look on Willa's face nearly stole Bruce's heart. She was trying so hard. He knew the cost of that encouragement for her. Joe's success today meant success for her as well. A step she sorely needed, if she was going to be able to heal from the tragedy she'd endured. *Be with her,* he prayed. Then, sure God already knew what he was trying to say, he added, *She means a lot to me. They all do.*

He got down to Joe's level. "Just being willing to try is a brave thing, you know. I believe you can do this. But if you're not sure anymore, it's okay."

Joe's lips were pressed together tightly, but the kid stood up with the swagger of a superhero. He still had a coin in each hand, making Bruce wonder if he'd kept a grip on them all night. If you could measure courage per pound or per inch, the ratio for Joe would put the boy far above some of the most imposing athletes and soldiers Bruce had known. This kid had heart—and guts. Bruce didn't mind admitting he adored the little guy.

"Mom and Jack are gonna hold my coins," Joe announced.

Bruce nodded. "Good choice." He held out a hand to Joe. "Let's do this."

They joined the other kids at the edge of the pond, where Bruce went through his usual pre-lesson routine. "Everyone feeling well and healthy?"

"Yes!"

"Any storms in the sky?"

"No."

"Everyone have a buddy?"

Everyone already had a buddy from earlier lessons, so Joe looked up at Bruce with concern.

"I'm your buddy, Joe."

The declaration made the boy grin.

Those who needed life jackets strapped them on, Joe included. When everyone was ready, they waded into the water inside the buoys Bruce had set up on the first day. As the level rose to Joe's ankles, he heard the boy say, "It's only water. I'm okay," over and over. Today was supposed to be about floating on their backs and learning proper kicking technique, but it was clear no one wanted to do anything but cheer Joe on.

Taking a last look at Willa, who had moved with Jack as close to the pond as he'd ever seen her since

Joe's fall, Bruce hunched down into the water in front of Joe. "You got this. Up to your knees."

Fists tight, eyes on Bruce, Joe repeated, "It's just water. I'm okay," as he took more steps into the pond. He wobbled a little when he hit an unsteady patch under the water, but he kept going.

"Okay, now, up to your waist," Bruce called out. He moved in front of Joe and held his hands out on the surface of the water. "Reach out to my hands when you feel yourself start to float."

"That's it!" the other kids cheered from a few feet away. "Look at you!"

"Come on, Joe!"

It was as if the whole world held its breath until Joe took the final step that sent him bobbing in the water. His eyes went wide as his feet left the pond bed. Bruce heard a small yelp from the shore, where he could see Willa's hands clutching her chest out of the corner of his eye. He felt Joe's hands lock on to his as the boy tilted forward into a swimming position.

"Okay, now kick," he encouraged Joe. "I got you. You know how. Little small kicks, like we did that other day on the shore to make splashes." He could feel his face breaking into a wide smile. "You're doing it, Joe. You're swimming."

"I'm swimming!" came Joe's victory cry. Bruce felt it light up every corner of his chest. Every corner of his soul. "I'm swimming!"

It was then that he noticed every single member of the staff and all the guests had gathered on the shore and were cheering wildly. "Look at you, Joe. You're swimming!"

When the boy's face finally broke into a smile as wide as his own, Bruce said, "You ready to let go and swim on your own?"

"Yeah," Joe said with determination. "Lemme go."

"Okay." Bruce spread his fingers and let Joe's hands slip from his. It was probably far more like a doggy paddle than how most children Joe's age swam, but it was still the most beautiful thing Bruce had ever seen in the water.

Once released, Joe attacked the water with wild, joyful enthusiasm. "I'm swimming!" He bobbed around, making whooping noises as the crowd cheered.

"Yes, you are!" Bruce swam around him, making just as much noise as anyone else. Then, overcome with the emotion of the moment, Bruce swept him up in a great big hug, swirling the pair of them around in the water in what had to be the world's wettest victory celebration. The splashes felt like fireworks, and Joe's happy giggles made Bruce's heart soar. "You're swimming, Joe. You got your brave face. I'm so proud of you." He couldn't help but hold the boy close, soaking in the happiness of the moment.

Within seconds, they were surrounded by splashing, cheering kids celebrating Joe's victory. They swam around for a few minutes more, even stopping to wave at Willa and Jack, who offered enthusiastic waves back. Bruce knew he'd remember this moment for the rest of his life, as would Joe.

Bruce caught the boy's gaze, green eyes sparkling even more brilliantly than the sun on the pond's waves. "You did it."

"Yep." Joe bobbed in the water like a baby duck, his

arms and legs working just as furiously to move himself through the water. Utter victory and happiness burst from every part of his small, wet, delightfully squirmy body.

Bruce scooped him up to carry the boy on his shoulders, raising him out of the water with a loud whoop like the hero Joe was. He walked onto the shore like he was walking on air. Given the sight of Willa's tearfully happy smile, maybe he was.

It was the complete opposite of the last time he'd hauled Joe out of the water. The boy scrambled out of his grip the minute Bruce set him down, only this time Joe flung himself, wet and happy, into his mother's arms. "I did it! I swam in the pond, Mom! I wasn't scared at all." Then, as if he could read Bruce's thoughts, he added, "Well, maybe just a little bit at first."

"That's why there are two sides to the coin," Bruce added, remembering that fear wasn't a weakness—it was part of the victory.

Willa's expression said a dozen things at once. Relief, gratitude, joy…and something he very dearly hoped was affection. He'd taken so much from Willa. It was healing to be able to give this big thing back to her. He knew that Joe's victory was a victory for her as well. Joe's courage would bolster her own.

If Mason was right—and Bruce was sure he was— Camp True North Springs was a place where God showed up in amazing ways to heal wounded families. Knowing he'd been part of this healing for Willa and the boys sank deep into his heart. A bit of their new hope found its way into his own soul, too. Maybe the wonders of Camp True North Springs weren't just for the guest families.

Above her son's soaking embrace, Willa reached out to grip Bruce's hand. "Thank you." He could tell she wanted to say more, and he wanted to say so much more than *You're welcome.* It tangled his emotions to feel so much connection and so much distance between Willa and himself all at the same time. What was the future of all that complication? Was there one at all?

"I want my coin," Joe declared to Willa with a *This is important* tone.

"You gonna throw it in?" Jack asked. It was clear to Bruce—and likely even clearer to Willa—that the boy envied his brother's very public accomplishment. Bruce's prediction that Jack wouldn't be far behind Joe into the water would likely come true. That was probably the reason for the taint of fear he could still see in Willa's eyes.

"I get to now," Joe said, holding out his hand to his mother.

"You do indeed," Bruce replied.

Willa removed the coin from her pocket and placed it carefully in Joe's palm. Did she place the *Courage* side up on purpose, or was that just a happy accident? *I don't think there are any accidents here,* Mason's words reminded him.

"You all gotta come," Joe said. "Out on the dock with me."

The dock where he'd fallen. The dock Willa or Jack had never set foot on. Did Joe know what he was asking? Bruce raised an eyebrow at Willa, silently asking *You okay with that?* while he tried to plot a way out for her if she wasn't. The world had asked enough of that woman for one day—he'd cover for her any way he could if she wasn't up to it.

She raised her chin in an echo of the woman he'd discovered on the porch, the photograph that had become his all-time favorite. She took hold of Jack's hand, and Bruce was startled by how much he wished she'd taken his.

"Of course we'll come," she said.

And with that, the four started toward the dock.

Willa didn't remember her steps out onto the dock. They were a blur of happiness and fear and people offering congratulations and a few knowing looks from the other moms. She had Jack by one hand and Joe by the other, acutely aware of how close each boy was to the edge of the dock and the slightly-less-treacherous water below.

Willa felt, rather than saw, Bruce walking behind them. His support was like a physical sensation gently coming near. She was grateful she had a son in each hand, for the urge to reach out and grab hold of the support she could feel coming from Bruce was almost too strong to resist. It was nearly impossible to fathom how much she'd disliked the man when they'd first met. How had she ever taken such an instant aversion to him? His profession wasn't any reason to judge him. How very much like God to use a photograph to show her how to rediscover her courage.

They reached the edge of the dock, jutting perhaps a dozen feet out into the pond. The bottom of the pond could be seen from here, and yet it still felt hundreds of feet deep. Precarious and looming. What was it Joe had kept repeating? *It's just water. I'm okay.* Maybe it worked to calm people slightly *older* than six.

"What do I do?" Joe leaned all too calmly to one side of the dock in order to talk to Bruce, who was still behind them.

He came up around them, grabbing Willa's shoulders to steady her as he edged himself toward the front. Even fresh out of the water, his hands were warm and strong. She noticed the contact far more than she ought to. His momentary closeness felt just as risky as her sons' nearness to the water. She was on the edge of something with this man, but unsure—or perhaps just unwilling—of how to name what it was.

"Put it in the water any way you want," Bruce answered. "Throw it or let it drop. Whatever feels like saying goodbye to that old fear."

"You should throw it super far," Jack suggested.

"Jack…" Willa chided him. It should be Joe's moment.

"That gets to be your decision," Bruce said.

Joe looked up at Bruce. Admiration filled her son's eyes. "*You* could throw it super far."

Bruce smiled, clearly touched by the offer. "I could, but it's something you should do." For just a moment, Bruce caught her eyes with the smile still on his face. There was such a warmth about him today. Something so opposite from the chill of fear that had followed her for too long. That first day, he had told her that this pond was the perfect place to overcome their fears. *He was right,* she thought, feeling a smile steal across her own face.

"Okay," Joe said, turning the coin over. The coin had seemed small in Bruce's hands but enormous in Joe's palm. "Here goes." With a hearty shout of "Goodbye, scared of water!" Joe flung the coin high into the air out over the pond.

Willa felt her heart sail with the coin as it arced over the water. It was a sizable throw for a boy Joe's age. She supposed other people heard the plop it made as it hit the water as a small sound, but it had the crash of a tidal wave to her ears. The sun caught the metal once or twice as it tumbled down toward the bottom, but then it disappeared into the weeds and depth. The crowd on the bank applauded as a circle of ripples spread out over the glistening water.

It was a small, silly thing. Then again, it wasn't small or silly at all. It was a creative, perfect way to help Joe embrace what he'd done. Willa let herself look at Bruce, to take in his tender and triumphant expression. He cared. A great deal. What an unexpected, powerful blessing that was. When he placed his hand on Joe's shoulder—something Rick would have done—the surge of emotion in her chest wasn't resentment or replacement; it was a deep gratitude for the man who'd become so much more than a swimming teacher…and—she could no longer ignore—a growing care for the man himself.

That care and gratitude doubled when Bruce made a point of putting a hand on Jack's shoulder as well. "Now you both found your brave faces while you were here."

Did Bruce realize what a gift that was? So many people treated the boys as a set, including both but forgetting how they were individual people. Bruce had managed to find ways to reach Jack and Joe in ways particular to them. She thought back to the first day, when Bruce had teased them about being able to trade places without him knowing, but that could never happen now. In his words to Jack, Bruce let Jack know that he didn't have to swim just because Joe did.

But he might. Willa couldn't escape the feeling that God had sent the one man who could make a way back into the water for them all. Something she would have declared impossible mere weeks ago. Of all the people in all the world, who should have been standing out on this dock, doing what they were doing, these were the right four people.

And that was a dangerous thought. They were not a family. Not only was she far from ready for anything like that, but Bruce was not the kind of man to settle down to a family life. She'd be grateful if he stayed in the boys' lives—and something told her he likely would—but it could never come to anything more.

"Anyone for courage cookies?" Chef Seb called out from a table set under the shade of a nearby tree.

"'Courage cookies'?" Jack asked with a wrinkled nose, as if courage were a vegetable.

"Well, actually, they're chocolate chip cookies, but I figured I'd call 'em *courage cookies* for today. Extra delicious, if you ask me."

Bruce actually gave Willa a dashing wink. "I think courage *should* taste like chocolate, don't you?"

Her laugh felt rich and full…and buoyant. Today she really did feel as if she could float on water. And if that wasn't worthy of a great chocolate chip cookie, what was?

Chapter Sixteen

The following evening, Willa couldn't help but think the pond looked beautiful. For the first time, she actually *enjoyed* looking at it. The boys were busy roasting even more marshmallows by the fire with Deborah and Nelly Collins, and Willa marveled at her sense of calm and treasured memories as she viewed the moon's silvery reflection in the ripples. *I will miss this place.*

I will miss more than just this place. She knew now that she would miss Bruce. *What do I do with that, Lord? It all feels right and wrong at the same time. I'm not ready to feel the things I'm starting to feel.*

Her silent pleas to God were interrupted by baby Olivia's wail. Willa turned to see Isabel had joined her on the grass beside the pond. The young mom looked weary.

"Please tell me at some point all the teeth come in?" She shifted her daughter to the other shoulder, and Willa noticed a large patch of damp on Isabel's shirt. Baby Olivia was indeed drooling up a storm—and crying up one as well.

She remembered long nights of her and Rick walking the floor with not just one teething baby boy but two. There were weeks she thought she'd never see a full night of sleep ever again.

"They do," she commiserated, "but it takes far longer than you'd like."

"William was so much better at staying calm when she got like this." Grief weighed down Isabel's words.

Compassion filled Willa's heart, and she held out her hands for the infant. "Here, let me take her for a bit."

Isabel hesitated. "She might fuss more."

Offering a smile, Willa replied, "She might fuss less on a calmer shoulder. And you deserve a break." Isabel gently shifted Olivia into Willa's arms. The child fussed for a minute, then looked up at Willa with red-rimmed but curious eyes. "There's a trick Rick's mom taught me when Jack and Joe were teething. Do you mind if I try it?"

"You can try anything," Isabel moaned.

Willa took her finger and worked it into Olivia's tiny mouth, easily finding the swollen spot on the baby's gum. She began gently rubbing and pressing where the new molar was pushing up and making the child miserable. Olivia startled, but Willa made shushing sounds and rocked while she kept pressing. Eventually, the baby settled down, letting Willa rub, and softened her sweet pink lips around Willa's finger.

"Teach me how to do that," Isabel said.

"You wouldn't think pressure would help, but it does. So does a frozen green bean, if you can get Chef Seb to give you some."

Isabel laughed, and together the two women soaked in the sudden silence.

"I'm amazed at you," Isabel said. "I don't know how you did it. Joe in the water again and all, I mean." She sighed. "I wouldn't have it in me."

Willa managed a soft laugh. "I'm not sure I had it in me, to be honest. Water and I... Well, we didn't get along." It was more than that. Water had somehow turned into an enemy. The horrid monster that took Rick from her. But looking out over the pond tonight, Willa could toe up to the idea that water was just...water. In fact, she'd said the words *didn't get along* rather than *don't get along* without even realizing it. That felt like the beginning of healing.

Isabel looked down at the grass and shifted her weight. "Can I ask you something?"

"Sure." It was odd to note how the young woman seemed to look up to her. Willa hadn't felt admirable in a long time. Perhaps that was why Bruce's admiration struck such a chord in her. She knew it went deeper than admiration—and what should she do about that?

"How long did it take before you felt like you wouldn't be alone from here on in?"

While Willa had an idea what the woman was really asking, she replied, "What do you mean?"

Isabel gave a small whimper worthy of her daughter. "I feel so alone. My mom helps and friends do what they can, but it's not the same. No one is William. No one could be. But I can't stay like this forever. I don't want to stay like this forever. Olivia needs a whole family. A woman from my support group says it takes two years to heal from losing a spouse." She tugged on a lock of her long, dark hair. "I don't think I can last that long."

Willa remembered those desperate early days. All

the helpful friends and relatives in the world couldn't fill the giant gaping hole in her heart. She'd needed the twins desperately but also felt so drained of love she worried she couldn't do right by them. "I don't think there are any rules here. No timelines. Certainly no formula to make it easier." With a tiny puff of maternal pride, Willa noticed Olivia had fallen asleep in her arms. Ah, the bliss of a finally sleeping baby. "Why ask me?"

"You seem like you've got it together."

Willa would have laughed out loud at that had it not been for fear of waking Olivia. "Oh, I don't. I thought everyone could see that."

"What everyone can see, if you don't mind my saying, is how Bruce has a thing for you."

When Willa felt her eyes pop wide, the young mom clamped a hand over her mouth and said, "Was I not supposed to say that? My mouth gets me into such big trouble."

Willa couldn't come up with an answer. She hoped the dark night hid the flush now heating her cheeks.

"I just wanted to know how you know it's okay to think...to feel like that. When..." Embarrassment rushed the woman's words. "There was a man in our church who asked me to dinner, and I thought I'd be sick on the spot. I wanted to scream, 'How can you even ask me that?' I don't want to feel like that forever. I still love William, but I'll *always* love William. How does it all mesh together?"

Willa finally found some words to capture what she knew Isabel was trying to say. "You mean, being so lonely but not ready to let anyone into your life?"

"Yeah. That. Exactly that."

"Deborah Collins told me you're never really ready. I think she called it 'a cliff you have to make yourself jump off.' Deborah has a vivid way of putting things, that's for sure."

"Are you going to? Jump off that cliff?"

If Olivia had not been sleeping so soundly, Willa might have been tempted to pass the child back and make a quick exit up to the house. "With Bruce?" Even putting words to that idea made her pulse jump. When Isabel nodded, Willa could only answer, "I don't know. There are a million reasons not to."

Isabel's sigh was full of memory. "There were a million reasons not to fall for William. None of them ever ended up mattering."

"I'll admit, it's nice to feel something." Willa quickly corrected, "A *tiny bit* of something. But his life is far too different from mine for anything to work."

"Your boys adore him. And he's gotten both of them to make huge strides. That's got to be worth something."

"I do think it'd be nice if he stayed in touch with them. He'd be a pretty cool hero of a friend for a boy their age to have." Bruce had said he would do as much, and the gifts he'd given felt like a promise to stay in their lives. A tiny part of her wanted to know he'd stay in her life, too, but it couldn't be anything romantic.

"So you wouldn't run off screaming into the night if he asked to dinner." Isabel pushed out a breath, seeming to assume something Willa didn't think she'd said.

"Well…"

"Thanks. It's nice to know I'll get there someday."

She slanted a sideways glance at Willa. "So would you say yes if he asked? I mean, just theoretically?"

An awful thought came to Willa. "Did he put you up to this?" It seemed a stunt more suited to the schoolyard than a man of Bruce's experience.

"Gosh, no. There I go, saying the wrong thing again. I think I just want to know. If you can get there, I can get there someday. Plus, you can't argue the man is easy on the eyes and a nice guy to boot."

Bruce was handsome. And while his character was intense, he was admirable. If God had placed him in her life at any other time, she might act on what she was beginning to feel. But not now. There was no room in her life for a man who roamed the world, looking for the next dangerous adventure.

"I would say no," she finally replied to Isabel. Then, with a surprising sideways glance of her own, she added, "But I would be very flattered."

Mason put a hand on Bruce's shoulder Wednesday afternoon. "This is what it's all about, Bruce. I'm so glad you stayed. I promise you'll never forget this."

"So you keep saying." Mason's excitement over the day of the flower ceremony seemed over the top. Bruce had never remembered Mason as being such a sentimental man. Evidently, love did that to a guy.

It had renewed Bruce's faith to see the strength of Mason and Dana's love for each other. Truth be told, it had sparked a yearning in Bruce to have such a deep and abiding love in his own life. Always happy to be a roamer, Bruce was finding himself thinking about the benefits of having a home. *To know I belonged some-where. What would that feel like?*

"I'm really glad you're here to take pictures of this. In fact, I'm just glad you're here to see it." Mason walked over to a table under the tree, which had a bunch of different types of flowers laid out on it. "Get shots of this before everyone comes out. And then make sure you get shots of each family as they send the flowers out into the pond. If you stand over there—" he pointed to a spot a little farther down the circular bank of the pond "—you'll capture their faces." Mason put his hand to his chest. "It's their faces that always do me in."

This was starting to sound like a highly emotional event. Bruce wasn't sure he was ready for that. Sure, he'd photographed dozens of dramatic events, captured all sorts of people in highly emotional states. But those were of strangers. These were people he knew. That was going to make keeping an objective distance nearly impossible. Would that make his photos better? Or worse?

Dana came down off the porch with a pitcher of water, glasses and a dauntingly large box of tissues. "This is my favorite day of camp," she said as she set the items down next to the flowers. "Even with all the crying." She smiled at Bruce. "I'm so glad you're here to see this and get pictures. I always get too caught up in everyone to remember to take them."

Bruce finally worked up the nerve to ask, "Is this like a memorial service?"

"Yes and no," Mason said. "I keep trying to come up with a simple way to explain it, and I never do. Charlie does it best, so listen to him when he tells everyone what to do."

Dana looked back up toward the house. "Here they come." Remembering something, she ducked over to Bruce. "Did you get an okay from Willa to take their photos?"

Bruce felt a smile cross his features. "I did."

Her smile joined his. "I'm so glad to hear that. She's come a long way in her time here. You had a lot to do with that."

He could only shrug. "Maybe." He wanted to think he'd played a role in Willa's healing, but it felt wrong to claim that with the most important facts yet to be revealed. Bruce had almost convinced himself he could tell Willa about his role in Rick's death. Almost. Mostly because he knew that once she knew, he'd never be allowed to be part of her life ever again. And right now he was enjoying being part of her life—and the twins—too much to be able to give that up. *All these people think you're so brave. If they only knew what a coward you really are.*

Any such moping would have to wait as the families came down toward the pond. Bruce snapped shots of Deborah Collins and Nelly. He captured one of Champion Taylor's trademark goofy smiles as he came down across the grass with his mom, Vanessa. Carol and Arnie Owens each held one of young Marshall's hands, making for a heartwarming image.

Bruce's breath caught as he spied Willa coming down off the porch with Joe and Jack. His feelings toward those three were so strong he longed to put down the camera and just stare at them. He tried to remember the day he couldn't tell Jack from Joe. Now they were so distinct and cherished in his heart he couldn't imagine not knowing who was who.

And there was Willa. Even her walk had changed— she carried herself with a newfound grace and strength. His photographer's eye wished he'd been able to take pictures of her that first day so he could show her how much she'd changed. He could still see the remnants of anxiety as she got nearer the water, but like the coin he'd given Joe, he could also see the courage in her to face it. *What I wouldn't give to see the day when she isn't anxious at all,* he thought. Or maybe it was more like a prayer.

He'd fallen for Willa—for all three of them. Come to care so much it scared him. He had anxieties now, but they were about how life would feel without them around. Some part of him knew it would be a hollow and empty existence. Maybe, for a man who did what he did, that was for the best.

Willa caught his eyes for a second, and he felt that unnamable tug stretch between them even across the distance. *Think of it as a gift,* he told himself. *You get this tiny little bit with them before it all goes away. That has to be better than never getting it at all. That has to be enough.*

"Hi, everybody," Charlie greeted them as he stood next to the table. "This thing we do comes from my mom. She was from Hawaii, and they do this there to remember people. It feels hard—I get it—but it feels good, too." He picked up a beautiful pink flower, and Bruce snapped a few shots of him holding the bloom up for everyone to see. "You don't have to do it if you don't want to, but I hope you do. You just pick the flower that looks to you like the person you want to remember. Mom liked pink, so I always choose a pink one for her. But that's just me. There aren't any rules."

Bruce walked farther down the bank so that he had the right angle to capture Charlie as he walked out onto the dock. He could still hear Charlie clearly, which was good. Mason was right—he didn't want to miss a moment of this.

"We remember Mama," Charlie said as he knelt down and lovingly placed the bloom on the water. "I used to do her last, behind my grandparents, but today she gets to go first." With that, he tapped the flower gently, sending it on a journey across the ripples toward the center of the pond.

Bruce captured the bloom's voyage out over the sparkling waves. Pride at the memorable, compelling image welled in his chest. *This place is so important. Life-changing.* He knew, without a doubt, that his life had been changed.

As each family went through the ritual of selecting flowers, naming their lost loved ones and sending the blooms out onto the water, Bruce must have snapped a hundred shots. Even so, his best ones might never do the moments justice. Just like the balance of courage and fear he'd tried to teach Jack and Joe, the balance of sorrow and celebration radiated through the air.

It came as no surprise that Willa, Jack and Joe were the last ones to step up to the table. The surge of gratitude and honor to be here was so strong that Bruce had trouble making sure to take photos. The moment went so deep into his soul—his heart—that it stole his breath. He had one thought as Willa walked toward the dock with a brilliant blue flower in her hand: *this woman is extraordinary.* And he would let her know that, no matter what the cost to him turned out to be.

Chapter Seventeen

The simple task of picking up a flower off the table loomed huge and heavy. Part of Willa knew this was a healthy thing to do, that if she could push through the pain, there would be joy—or perhaps just release—on the other side. The therapist who had been working with Joe and Jack to help them process their grief told the story of C. S. Lewis's dragon, who'd needed to shed his crusty old scales to become something fresh and new. This felt so much like that. Both she and the boys needed to shed the old, brittle parts of themselves to move on to new things.

And for the first time she could remember since the drowning, Willa *wanted* to move toward new things. This place had pushed her forward out of the fog of bitter sorrow. *Thank you, Lord. Only You could deliver me to a camp I didn't want to visit and into water I refused to wade.*

She looked out onto the pond at that moment, her eyes finding Bruce as he stood a ways down the shore. He had his camera up to his eye, but it fell away as their gazes met. His expression said everything she was feeling, everything neither of them could quite yet say. *Thank you, Lord, for him. For what he's done for us.* She couldn't quite bring herself to thank God for what grew in her heart right now because it felt so dangerous and unreachable. If only they could have more time. If only they weren't both returning to their oh-so-different lives in a matter of days. It made her want to grasp these final hours and hold them tight like a treasure.

Is that okay, Rick? You would want my heart to heal, wouldn't you? Willa felt sure he'd want her life to be complete beyond his time in it. He'd want the boys to have a father figure in their life. It couldn't be Bruce, but she could come to a bittersweet thankfulness that Bruce had drawn her closer to whatever her future held.

The twins stood on either side of her, each holding the flowers they'd chosen. She'd worried the moment would feel heavy and difficult. Looking down into Jack's and Joe's beautiful green eyes—so very much like their father's—it wasn't heavy at all. It was hard, but that wasn't the same thing. The boys seemed to guess, as she did, that something sad would float away with the flowers, and something new would fall into its place.

"I'll go first," Jack said. Willa's affection at his raised chin and straight shoulders filled every corner of her heart. "We remember Daddy," he said clearly and loudly as he tossed the blue flower out onto the water. In a wonder Dana had said she never could explain, all the other flowers had begun to drift toward each other in the center of the pond. Jack's flower, however, seemed to hold still and wait for its two companions.

"We remember you, Daddy," Joe said, launching his flower out into the ripples with typical Joe enthusiasm. The boy who used to lunge himself fearlessly into the waves now sent his flower out in the same way. It made her smile even as a tear slipped down her cheek.

Willa let her bloom drop carefully into the water. "God bless you, Rick. You are always in our hearts." Something did indeed slip off her weary soul as the flower dipped into the water, its tiny splash pulling Jack's and Joe's blooms toward itself so that it made a little three-flower raft. There was a power in the knowledge that they floated together. Too much in her life had sunk. It was time to stay on the surface, to come up for air permanently.

She startled when Joe and Jack flattened themselves on the dock by some silent agreement and began to blow. Maybe they thought to fill imaginary sails to send the blooms out on their voyage. It made her laugh a little bit, and when she looked up at Bruce, his eyes were shining with the same joy. Sure enough, the trio of blooms began floating out to join the inexplicable raft of all the other flowers filling the center of the pond with color and memory.

When Dana had first explained the ceremony to her, she'd found the whole thing overblown and absurd. Now Willa couldn't imagine anything more perfect. Her, thinking a ceremony with water was perfect—only God could work such an astonishing thing.

It made her begin to wonder, against any logic or reason, what else God might be able to work in her life.

How long had it been since she'd viewed anything in her future with a sense of possibility?

Camp True North Springs had lived up to its promise of hope and healing. Her spirit lifted with the thought that the hard part was over.

Only it wasn't, for one harder part remained: the goodbyes. Watching Bruce make his way back around the arc of the pond bank, Willa knew her heart wanted far more than was wise where Bruce was concerned. She had the boys to think of, Bruce's dangerous profession, and the still-fragile state of their healing. And yet the glow in Bruce's eyes sparked such a welcome glow in her chest. That couldn't—or shouldn't—be ignored, should it?

He came up to her as the boys headed to the porch for the celebratory cake Chef Seb had made for the occasion. "Can we find some time later tonight? Just you and I? Before everyone goes home?" Bruce's voice was low and tentative. He looked sad, serious and sentimental— all things that barely belonged on his heroic features.

She could easily guess what he was going to say. After all, the same words were building up in her own heart. She should say no. Then again, perhaps this was a safe place to put a toe into that water. Here, in this grace-filled place away from ordinary life, she could try on the idea of feeling things for a man. Just for the handful of days they had left. Test out the slow opening of her heart to the possibility of new love.

For this could never be love—it was far too soon for that. Still, she felt a surprisingly deep affection for Bruce. Under other circumstances, that powerful care might have someday become love. That seemed worth exploring. Worth finding the courage to try.

"I'd like that."

She has to know. If you care for her at all, you owe her the truth.

The ball of ice and regret that sank into Bruce's stomach after the flower ceremony only grew larger as the sun went down. After tonight, he was sure he'd be banished from Willa's life, and from Joe's and Jack's. The burn of that loss made it hard to breathe, made it hard to dig deep enough to find the courage to do what he knew he had to do.

It struck Bruce as perfect—or maybe just more painful—that Willa had suggested meeting him in the pretty little memorial garden off to one side of the property. The garden's curving stone wall held bricks engraved with the names of loved ones lost by camp families. Bruce hoped being surrounded by those memorials would help him honor Rick's memory by owning up to his role in the man's death. One of the most beautiful and powerful spots on the camp's grounds was a good place for the admission and the goodbye Bruce knew would take place tonight.

The heat of the day had faded to a warm night, with just enough breeze to keep it comfortable under a starry sky. Behind him, he could hear the sounds of the gathering that happened every night around the camp's firepit: laughter, the occasional shout, and tonight Arnie Owens had pulled out his guitar and gotten everyone singing. Bruce sat on the stone wall, trying to pull in every detail. He'd need to make the memory of this night last for a very long time.

"Hi." Willa's voice came soft as a breeze as she stepped into the low glow of the tiny lights strung up around the garden. She had her arms wrapped around her chest despite the evening's warmth, tentative and delicate as a bird. Her eyes showed that she knew what he did. Meeting here tonight crossed a line they'd been trying very hard to deny was there. Being alone with her on purpose, without the boys, gave them no excuses or distractions. No way to hide what they were feeling. The sparkle in her eyes matched the terrified wonder in his own heart.

It would be easy—so easy—to admit the strength of what he felt about her. On the other hand, it would feel like pulling his heart out to tell her the truth he knew would destroy those feelings.

He would do both. He had made a solemn promise to himself and to God that he would. What happened after that had to be left to God's wisdom—and hopefully, His mercy.

"Hi." Bruce found his words balled up in his throat like some nervous schoolboy. He'd relished how the sunshine had made her so beautiful when he'd taken the portrait of her. Now, in the moonlight, Willa managed to look even more beautiful. Any doubt that he'd fallen hard for her vanished. What a double-edged sword it was that he'd lost his heart at the same time he'd lost his future with her.

Willa gestured back toward the glow of the campfire, flashing a sheepish smile. "Vanessa and Champion have the boys for an hour." The *so we can be alone* hung potent and unspoken between them.

An hour. He needed a year, a decade with this woman, and God was only granting him an hour. "Willa, there are two things you really need to know." It was important he made himself say that. Once he told her there were two things he needed to say, he wouldn't be able to go back on the second. No matter how hard it was.

As Bruce drew in a breath to start on the first, Willa held up a hand. "Wait." She pulled in a deep breath of her own and ventured a few steps toward him. There was an unexpected, slightly skittish sense of purpose in her movements. "Before you say whatever it is you wanted to say, I want to go first."

He hadn't expected that. Her declaration knocked his plans out of whack. *You can't go back on this,* he told himself. *But you can let her go first.* He nodded.

Her arms dropped to let her hands twist together, and Bruce fought the urge to reach out and envelop them in his own. "And I want your promise," she went on, "that you won't interrupt me until I've said everything I want to say. It's important."

"Okay," he replied. What could be on her mind to make her say something like that?

Willa shifted her feet, planting them solidly. She had a speech all teed up—he could see it in her features. He liked how well he could read her. Still, he could only half guess what might be coming.

"I was upset you were here that first day. It was as if everything that had caused me pain was wrapped up in what you were here to do. I mean, really, what are the odds? Water and swimming *and* photographs? To be honest, I felt like God was just being cruel."

You have no idea, Bruce thought.

"And then you pushed. In all the places I didn't want you to push. And the boys looked up to you *so much*. When you got them to do things I wasn't ready to push them to do, I resented you. I'm sorry for that. Even though I knew it was good for them, I resented your courage. It felt so unfair that you had all this strength while I didn't have any."

Bruce picked up a small rock beside him on the wall just to give his hands something to do. They were itching to reach for her. He'd promised not to interrupt, but he hadn't counted on it being this hard.

"I don't know when it happened, really. But suddenly, I started seeing you as this…gift. This person sent to pull me out of a place I thought I had to stay forever. You began to show me—and Jack and Joe—that we didn't have to be stuck in that dark, sad place. We could climb out of it. It was hard, but you were strong and you showed us how. Even when we stumbled, you showed us how to get up."

She took a step toward him, and it was as if all the air had left Arizona. Bruce's pulse thundered as he realized what she was saying, where her words were leading.

"I don't know how," she went on, her voice gaining power as she met his eyes. "I don't know why—and to be honest, it's really scary, but the truth is I…care for you. I care for you," she repeated, as if to proclaim it to the stars in case they hadn't heard the first time. "I thought my heart would stay hard and dark forever, but it hasn't. You opened it." Her cheeks flushed, and Bruce felt their heat rise in his own chest. "Even when I fought it—fought you—tooth and nail, you opened my heart."

Bruce hadn't even realized he'd risen to his feet when she took a step closer. She was within arm's reach now, and every cell in his body was reeling from how close she was. He ought to stop her, but he couldn't bring himself to do it.

"You say I have courage. I don't feel like I do, but you make me feel like I could. So I'm going to try and find that courage, just for tonight, and be that woman you claim you see."

With that, she leaned in and kissed his cheek. Softly, with so much cautious tenderness it took his breath away. "I care for you, Bruce," she whispered against his cheek.

Where was all his legendary strength now? He was helpless not to give in to the sweet brush of her lips, powerless not to return the kiss with all the longing that had been building over the past several days. This would be the only moments of care he would get with her, and he would relish every bit of them. He wrapped his arms around her, marveling in how she softened against him, how exquisite she felt within his embrace.

She had it all wrong. It was *she* who was the gift to *him*.

One he hardly deserved.

Chapter Eighteen

I never thought...

It wasn't even really a coherent thought, more a wave of emotion, as Willa softened against the strength of Bruce's kiss and his embrace. She'd been so sure she could never feel this way again—certainly not yet. It ought to feel rushed and wrong and maybe even disloyal to Rick's memory, but it didn't.

It felt precious and right and unspeakably tender. A single moment in time she would hold on to forever. She felt that same grasping in Bruce's touch. A desperate urge to hold on, to stretch this perfect moment out beyond the limits they both knew were there. Real life wasn't on their side, but that didn't stop tonight from being a wonderful, healing gift.

She'd had the courage to tell him how she felt about him, to offer that wild dare of a kiss. And it hadn't blown up in her face—just the opposite. It had given her, given them, this moment.

Bruce pulled away just far enough to gaze into her eyes as he ran one hand gently down her cheek. She hadn't even realized tears had come, but she wasn't embarrassed—the moment was so full of emotion for both of them. "I'm glad I found my courage," she whispered, laying her head against his chest. It felt perfectly safe to be here with him. She knew it was just for this moment, but that was all she could bear right now, anyway. There was no viable future for them together, but Bruce had opened her heart, and she'd find a way for that to be enough.

"Me too." Bruce kissed her forehead and pulled her even closer. Willa felt something so close to love—so startlingly, impossibly close to love—that it left her dizzy.

She tilted her head to look up at him. "Turns out I have a brave face, too."

"You have a lovely, beautiful brave face." His hand traced the curve of her cheek. "I care so much about this face. I care so much about you."

Willa felt like she had to say it, had to remind the both of them. They couldn't be starry-eyed kids about this. "It's just for now. While we're here."

"I know," he whispered as he settled her against his chest again. "I know."

He stroked her hair. It was such a sweet, wistful gesture. Wildly out of character for the rugged adventurer.

"Willa," he said, his voice exquisitely gentle.

Somehow the way he said her name echoed everything she was feeling. *I'm glad to know this part of him.* Did he realize what a gift that was to her, how it healed scars she'd been sure would close up her heart forever?

They stood there in each other's arms for a long time, soaking in every detail of the moment. *Remember this,* she told herself. She gathered the sensations like treasures—how he touched her hair, the strong curve of his muscular arms, what the wild beat of his heart felt like under her palm. She held tight to the wondrous surprise of knowing she could care for a man again, and of knowing that new and delicate care was safe in his keeping.

It was the first time in so very long that no shred of fear loomed along the edges of her thoughts. *Hope,* Willa realized with a burst of clarity. *He's given me hope.* It made her heart glow and a smile come to her face.

"What did you want to tell me?" she asked, still smiling as she closed her eyes with her cheek against his chest.

"I came here determined to tell you how I felt about you. Whether you felt the same way or not, I didn't want to leave here without you knowing how much I care for you."

He cared for her. She knew that by his actions, of course, but it was such a gift to hear him say it. To know that this kind of care—the man–woman kind of care—was not gone from her life forever was such a blessing. Even if only a momentary one.

It made her delightfully curious what else he had come to say. He'd said he had two things to tell her. She couldn't imagine what else could make tonight any more special, but tonight was full of opportunities and possibilities. "What else?"

There was a shift in him, an almost imperceptible flinch. "Not yet," he said.

The sadness in his tone snagged her awareness, and Willa opened her eyes. "Bruce, what?"

His embrace tightened. "Give me just a bit. A moment more."

She understood the impulse. An hour wasn't nearly enough. The time they had left at camp wasn't nearly enough. Still, it would have to be.

Finally, with a sense of surrender that didn't really make sense, Bruce took her hand and pulled the two of them toward the wall. He motioned for her to sit down and did so as well, but with a bit of distance between them. When she reached for his hand, he shook his head. The earlier gentleness of his hands had disappeared. Instead, his fingers went back and forth between nervous flexing and tightly balled fists.

After what they'd just shared, what could be so hard to tell her? The cold tendril of fear she'd been so grateful to leave behind crept back into her spine. "Bruce, what is it?"

He didn't look at her, fixing his gaze on the ground between his feet. "I need to tell you something."

He didn't need to say the something was hard or even horrible—it was clear in his voice. Willa's pulse started to race. She tried to think of something supportive to say despite the chill that went through her. Suddenly, the night didn't feel as warm, the dark not as soft. "I'm listening."

"The night Rick died. The night Rick drowned." She could see him force himself to use that terrible word, squinting his eyes shut as he did. Why would he bring that up now? She couldn't think of what to say, so she stayed silent, letting him find whatever words he needed to continue.

Finally, after an endless silence, he said, "I wasn't there."

Willa blinked, grasping for whatever connection he was making. "I know."

"No," he countered with a quick, sharp word, "I *wasn't there.* I was *supposed* to be. But I wasn't."

Her hand rose to her forehead, puzzling over his words. "I don't understand."

Bruce got up and began to walk slowly around the small circle of light still glowing in the garden. His hands were balled into tight fists at his side. "I was assigned to cover that harbor that day. To shoot the storm. My bureau chief had almost always given me those because he knew my background. I knew the coasts, the tides, that sort of thing. I suppose he thought it helped."

Willa still didn't see where this was going. But a tiny shrill voice at the back of her mind asked, *What if you had been there?* Could someone with Bruce's skills have saved Rick? They'd told her no, but would someone with his courage have gone into the water when no one else would? Those were unfair questions, but that didn't stop them from tightening her throat. They kept her from saying anything, even though she wasn't even sure Bruce was listening.

He finally looked at her, a chilling lost look in his eyes. "Do you remember the other storm? The one the week before?"

"Yes." A storm even worse than the one that had taken Rick had drenched the coast the week before. Piers had been damaged, boats tossed like toys, and everyone was reminded of what a storm surge was and how far its fury could reach. It was why Rick had been adamant about moving the car and why she'd been so worried about him doing so.

"I was sent to cover the pier damage two towns over. The national affiliate wanted dramatic shots of waves crashing against the pilings, that sort of thing. I went. I always went. I'd never turned down a risky assignment, never saw the need to. I knew how to handle myself around dangerous currents, so I always told myself I could get better shots than anyone else. I think I thought I was invincible, you know?"

Of course Bruce thought himself invincible. How could he live the life he did without such an attitude? "We all think we can't be harmed," she replied. "Until we are." She thought of Joe, flinging himself into waves far taller than his tiny self. "Fearless isn't really such a good thing."

Willa still didn't see what this had to do with how Rick had died. Bruce already said he hadn't been covering the harbor where Rick was. She couldn't grasp why Bruce looked so stricken, so tortured by his own words.

"All of a sudden, there was someone in the water. I remember thinking, 'You idiot,' until I heard his cry for help. The sound went right through me. Then I thought, 'You're not here because you know water, you're not here to be a photographer, you're here because you can save him.'"

Bruce glanced in her direction, but she could tell he was really seeing that coastline years ago. "I had done it before. I'd pulled drowning people from the water. I put down my gear and went in after him. I mean, that's what lifeguards do, right?"

Willa didn't know how to respond. Was he really

going to tell her about how he'd saved a drowning man
knowing that was how she lost Rick?

"I didn't. I had him for a second or two. But he panicked and began kicking and thrashing. I couldn't keep
a hold on him. Not with the waves the way they were.
I got tossed hard against one of the pier pilings, and
when I came up, he was gone."

He was gone. Those words tolled in her heart like
a mournful bell. *He's gone.* She'd gasped those same
words when Rick slipped under the waves that final time.

"I lost it," Bruce said, his back now to her. "I barely
made it back to shore, but I was so shook it was hours
before I could drive home. I'd never lost anyone before.
I was so sure, and I'd been so wrong. I was a mess for
a couple of days."

He turned to her then, and the hollow, awful look
in his eyes snapped the facts together for her. *Oh, Father God, no.* Her hand went up to her throat. She knew
what he was going to say next. The growing awareness
made Willa feel as if she was being swept out to sea
on dry land.

"I was assigned to cover the harbor where Rick was.
I turned it down. The first assignment I turned down
in my whole life would have put me there. I knew it the
minute I saw the footage on the news. It was exactly
where *I* was supposed to be. I might have saved Rick,
but I was too scared to try." His voice broke. "I should
have been there."

The shock of what he was saying made Willa nearly
dizzy. "You've known," she gasped out, "who we were.
The *whole time.*" Suddenly, his strange reaction to seeing her the first day made sense.

He didn't just represent the press she resented—
he *was* it. He was the target of the *Why don't you put
down your cameras and* do *something?* yelling that had
lodged in her chest for years. Willa's lungs burned with
the impossible idea that he'd made a choice that pre-
vented him from saving Rick. Whether or not it made
logical sense didn't matter. Whether Rick's death truly
was a direct result of Bruce's choice didn't matter. "This
whole time," she repeated, unable to stop the angry
shock rising up in her like a storm surge.

"Yes."

Bruce's one word had so much weight, it felt as if it
would sink the both of them to the bottom of the sea.

Willa stared at him for a long moment, eyes brim-
ming with tears and anger at the same time.

There should be something he could say, some way
to pull this moment back from the dark place it had
left them. There wasn't. No matter how sorry he was,
I'm sorry couldn't come close to redeeming the past or
changing what he'd done—or in this case, failed to do.

After a long and agonizing stretch of silence, Willa
made a sad muffled sound and then walked back across
the grounds toward the glow of the fire.

She walked away.

How could she do anything other than walk away?
There was no coming back from this. It felt fitting that
he was left in the dim glow of the garden lights, surrounded by the vast darkness of the Arizona night.
Bruce felt cold despite the warm air. He felt hollow
despite how her kiss had filled him moments before.

You knew it would be like this. She had to know, and

now she does. The debt hanging over his head these past few years was now paid. Bruce had been sure he knew how painful it would be, but he was wrong. It would have been painful in any case, but the depth of care he felt for Willa made it so much worse. And yet that care is what forced him to tell her. He cared too much *not* to tell her.

There was a coastal phenomenon that often happened just before storm surges. Hours before the giant tide came in, it went out. Far, far out. Whole harbors would drain, showing sand and rocks and sea bottom that was normally underwater. It made for an eerily fascinating landscape, which always seemed to pull unknowing on-lookers far out into dangerous territory. That curiosity got them killed when the monster tide surged back in with lethal speed.

Bruce felt like that. He'd been drained far beyond normal limits, emptied out and exposed. Something no one should be around. People's fascination with him was wrong and dangerous.

Bruce wasn't sure how long he just stood there, star-ing at the glow of the fire, which now seemed a mil-lion miles away. *Leave,* he told his feet even when they refused to move. *You've lost the right to be here. You knew tonight would end like this.* He did. He always had. He just never expected it to begin with the won-der of Willa's kiss.

He had gear back in the big house, but he couldn't bring himself to head that way. Instead, once he finally got his feet to move, he headed toward his car.

Mason called to him just as he put his hand to the

vehicle door. "Bruce!" The man was dashing toward him with the gear Bruce had left behind.

Gear or no, Bruce didn't want to answer. He didn't want to talk to anyone right now. He didn't want to see anyone—especially Mason, whose tragic life had now become such a blessing. That kind of redemption was far beyond his own life now. He pulled open the car door, determined to get inside and drive away.

"Bruce!" Mason's one hand grabbed his shoulder as he slid the bag of gear to the ground at Bruce's feet. Bruce wanted to whack Mason's hand away, to pull away from whatever friendly advice Mason might have. "What happened?" Mason asked, still winded from the sprint across the parking lot. "Willa looks a wreck. So do you."

Bruce turned. "What were you expecting? There was no happy ending to this story. There never was." A cold corner of his heart was turning from sad to angry. His chest burned like someone was holding a hot brand to it. Now he had such a vivid picture of the happiness that would never be his.

"So you told her."

"I said I would. I knew I had to. I just didn't count on…her."

Mason pushed the car door back shut, a silent declaration that he wasn't letting Bruce leave. At least not without a better explanation. "Meaning what?"

Bruce hadn't planned on telling anyone, but somehow it pushed its way past his resistance. "I care *so much* about her. And the boys."

"I could see that. Probably even before you figured

it out. It's why you had to tell her the truth. I get that. You did the right thing."

"Did I?" The words came out of him sharp and bitter.

"Didn't you?" Mason asked, looking puzzled.

"She kissed me," Bruce admitted as if it explained everything. "I was gearing up to tell her everything and she stopped me. She launched into this anxious, adorable speech about how she cares about me. About how the boys care about me. And then she kissed me." It still made no sense, but even now the memory of what it had felt like to hold her rushed through him. An astounding happiness that couldn't be his beyond that one moment. Whoever had said the bit about it being better to have loved and lost couldn't have felt like this.

How Mason could manage a knowing smile at that, Bruce couldn't fathom. "She really does feel the same way about you," his friend said. "I thought so—we all did—but pretty much no doubt about that now, is there?"

Bruce leaned against the car. "It makes it all so much worse."

Mason cocked his head. "Are you sure?"

Bruce glared at him. "Of course it does. I'd have been so much better off if she just kept resenting me. I can't care about her after what I did to her life. We can't get past this."

"Bruce, I don't think…"

He didn't want to hear Mason's faith-filled optimism right now. "Don't you get it? I choked. I refused an assignment for the first time in my life, and it kept me from being there when I could have saved Rick. I as much as let Rick drown with my own cowardice.

There's no forgiving that. I saw her eyes. She won't, and she shouldn't."

Now Mason glared at him. "That's what you believe?"

"It's what I *know*. It's what I've lived with every day since then. Why do you think I went to Africa? And all those other places? I needed to get away from what I'd done in Fort Lauderdale." Bruce was suddenly so tired, so weighed down. If he walked into the pond right now, he was certain he'd sink to the bottom.

Mason grabbed his arm. "You were being human. A man who went through something awful when you couldn't save that guy at the pier the week before. Come on, you told me you had nightmares for a month after that. You can't just turn around from something like that and do it all over again the next week just because your boss asked you to."

"I should have. Those boys would have their father today if I did."

"You don't know that," Mason shot back, shaking the arm he was holding. "You've always been a bit of an ego dude, but even *you* can't save everyone. I saw the news about that day. Whole cars were swept out to sea. You might not have even made it out alive." Mason shook his head. "And yet you're here. Here, now, where she is. You gotta wonder what God's hand is in all of this."

That was exactly the point Bruce couldn't swallow down anymore. "God's hand isn't *anywhere* in this. Just pain and loss and…" He yanked the car door back open and reached down to grab the gear bag. "I gotta go."

Mason stopped him. "This isn't over, Bruce. It's a mess, but that's what happens up here. Come back tomorrow. We'll figure a way through this."

"There is no way through this. At least now I know I've owned up to it." What did you do with your life once you admitted to the unforgivable? Bruce felt like there must be someplace he ought to turn himself in, some eternal penance he ought to be assigned. Still, what could be more of an eternal penance than a life without Willa? Without Jack and Joe?

"You're smarter than this, Bruce. What happened to Rick isn't your fault. It's not. It's sad and terrible, but it's not your fault. How can I get you to see that?"

Bruce pulled out of Mason's grasp. "That's just it. It doesn't matter what I see." He nodded back toward the fire, wishing he could get one last look at Willa. "It's what she sees. And now that will never change."

Before his friend could put up any more of his hopeful arguments, Bruce tossed the gear bag into the passenger seat and got into the car. He paid no attention to whatever Mason tried to say and started his car's engine. With a breath that felt like his last, Bruce drove off through the gates of Camp True North Springs with no intention of ever coming back.

Chapter Nineteen

The sun was just coming up when Willa roused the boys and got them dressed to head over to the camp kitchen. What probably looked like a stunning Arizona sunrise to other people was just a backdrop to her. The end of a hard night and the announcement of an even harder day.

She was grateful to find Chef Seb and his family already busy in preparations for breakfast. It was a sweet scene, with Seb's wife, Kate; her young daughter, Kimmy; and her older son, Kent, all helping out. The scents and sounds took her back to lazy Saturday mornings when Rick would occupy the boys by making waffles so she could grab a bit of extra sleep. She'd had almost no sleep last night, tossing and turning over the stinging turn life had taken in the last twelve hours.

Kate, in the instinctual fellowship of sleep-deprived mothers, handed Willa a coffee right away. "Rough night?"

"You could say so," Willa replied, not wanting to say more. She wasn't sure she could recount what had happened in the garden without the tears coming again.

There was no telling what would happen next, but the wee hours of the morning had assured Willa things could absolutely not be left as they were. She knew Bruce would not return to camp after what happened. How could she explain to the boys why Bruce left without saying goodbye?

She had to see Bruce again. And right now, there was only one way she could think of to make that happen. "No one else is up yet. Do you…um… Do you all know where Bruce lives? How far away?"

Seb turned off the standing mixer he was running with his stepson Kent and walked over to where Willa was standing. "Mason told me what happened last night."

Willa hated the idea of Seb knowing—but then again, it meant she didn't have to go through a painful explanation.

"We both know. I'm so sorry," Kate said. "He lives about two miles down toward town." She lowered her voice a bit to add, "Mason said he wasn't sure if he convinced Bruce to come back for today."

Seb reached into his pocket and pulled out a set of car keys. "Which means *you'd* better be the one to go to *him*. If you want to, that is." He held out the keys. "Do you?"

"I think so." Her feelings were such a mess she couldn't say for sure. She'd been reeling last night, thrown by the impossibility of what he'd told her. Still, now that the shock had receded, Willa had come to realize she had to see him again. She was sure her heart would tell her the truth of what to do, if she could just look into his eyes one more time.

Seb pressed his keys into Willa's hand. "Red Jeep.

Tags say 'CAMPCUK.' Tank's full." He pulled a paper towel off the roll. As he was writing an address down on it, he called over his shoulder, "Hey, Jack and Joe, have you ever had chocolate chip pancakes?"

"Sure!" the boys said in tandem.

"Well, today you're gonna help us make them while your mom goes on an errand for me. Okay by you?"

"Yep."

Kate pulled a travel mug down out of a cabinet and filled it with more coffee. She tucked Willa's arm into hers. "Let me tell you a quick story while I walk you to the car."

"Bring 'em back!" Seb's voice echoed into the hall as Willa and Kate made their way through the dining room to the big house's front door. "The guy *and* the Jeep!"

Kate laughed softly. "Seb was the last man I ever expected to come into my life after Cameron's death. I could list you a hundred reasons why it shouldn't have worked." A warm glow took over her eyes. "But it did. Not perfectly at first—not by a long shot—but that's what grace is for, hmm?"

"I don't know." It seemed like the only thing Willa could say about anything.

"I think you're right not to let it go just yet. He's hurt way more than any of us knew. You've been hurt. I thought the same thing about Seb and me, too. That we were each of us too damaged to make any kind of healthy whole."

Willa shook her head. "It's not really the same thing with Bruce and me." All the logic she could muster seemed useless in the face of everything she was feeling.

"I don't know. I mean, does the kind of pain and damage really matter when it's that big between two people? Pain is pain. Loss is loss. You either choose to find a way through it or you don't. Everyone here knows that. You do, too."

That was just it. She had to choose to find a way through it. She thought she had, finding the courage to tell Bruce how she felt. And then it had all fallen to such awful pieces. "It can't be possible to care about someone and resent them so deeply at the same time."

"Oh, I think it is." They'd reached the Jeep now, and Kate grinned at the bad joke of a license plate. "What I wanted to tell you was this—the whole time we were at camp, I thought I was saving Seb. That he needed me to rescue him. It wasn't until things got really bad that I realized he was saving me, too. I think sometimes God has to take us down to the bare bones to show us how much we really need each other."

Willa felt tears returning at the truth of Kate's words. "It's so hard. There's so much I don't know how to handle."

Kate pulled her into a hug. "I understand. I really do." She pulled away, giving Willa a serious look. "Do *you* believe Bruce is responsible for your husband's death?"

That was the big question, wasn't it? The one that had kept her up for hours, sorting through facts and feelings and fears. Praying for some kind of clarity. Now that someone had asked her out loud, Willa felt that clarity slowly rise to the surface. Like a bubble—small, frail but buoyant. "At first, I felt like it. But the more I thought about it, that's not the same thing as believing it. It hurts, and I'm still shocked, but no. I admit, I want someone to blame. It'd feel easier with someone to blame. But it's not Bruce."

Kate gave Willa's hand a squeeze. "He can't see that. And the man's drowning in guilt because of it. We can tell him all we want—and Mason certainly has—but the only person I think he'll believe that from is you. Maybe *you're* the one who saves *him.*"

Bruce stared at the email from his bureau chief. He'd had it up on his laptop for hours, fingers hovering over the keyboard to type a message asking for the assignment back. There was no point in keeping his promise to stick around now that things were so broken between him and Willa. A harrowing assignment in a combat zone suited his dark mood. He needed something all-consuming to drown out what he was feeling.

You're running away, he told himself for the tenth time. It was the only thing stopping him from sending the email. *It hasn't worked before now—what makes you think this time will be different?*

He stared at the battered Bible on his desk. He'd scoured it last night for some verse to confirm he'd done the right thing. If the truth really did set you free, he sure wasn't feeling it. It had come to him in the hours before dawn that what he really needed, the only path to the peace that eluded him, was forgiveness.

His head knew he had the forgiveness of God, his intellect understood that the price of his sins—no matter how massive—had been paid on the cross.

His heart ached for Willa's forgiveness. And that wasn't coming.

Bruce slammed the laptop shut and walked to his

balcony. He tried to let the rising sun's rays warm him, let the growing heat of the day steep some hope into his weary, aching body. *Are You trying to show me Your forgiveness is all I need?* he asked in prayer, feeling unable to grasp such a lesson. *Help me figure that out. You're gonna have to show me what to do next.* He knew his impulses—he was sure to make some bad decisions drowning in all this hurt. He shouldn't send that email. He shouldn't go anywhere reeling like this. And yet it seemed unbearable to stay. At least in forty-eight hours, Willa wouldn't be so achingly close. She and Jack and Joe would be back in Florida. Back home.

And where would he be? This wasn't home. Nowhere was home, really. There were just places, short-term rentals, with other people's furniture, where he lived in between assignments.

But Camp True North Springs had started to *feel* like home. Someplace he belonged. That pulled at him almost as much as Willa's sweet eyes and courageous, care-filled kiss.

Bruce let his head fall onto his arms as they rested on the balcony railing. *Why did You let me come here? Get to know her and the boys? It's all so much worse now that I care about them. I can't see the point in it.*

A red Jeep turned the corner and came down the otherwise-empty street. He recognized Seb's car and moaned, "Oh no." He did not need one of the chef's lectures right now. And if Seb knew, who else knew? The facts of his hand in Rick Scottson's death were bad enough when only he knew them. The more people knew what he'd done, the heavier the burden pressed down on him.

He should go inside, pull the blinds and pretend he hadn't seen the Jeep. Ignore the pounding Seb would give on his door, pretend to be asleep or, better yet, long gone. Only his car was in the driveway; Seb had likely seen him on the balcony, and that man was as relentless as the hot Arizona wind.

Seb did not get out of the car. Willa did.

He knew she could see him. But from this distance, he could not read her expression, nor could he guess why she'd come. His heart twisted in two—half-grateful to see her face again, half-fearful at the pain sure to come.

She stood, looking up at him from the driveway, wringing her hands. He gripped the balcony railing, suddenly bringing to mind how she'd gripped the big-house railing those first days at camp. She was this wondrous mixture of frailty and strength that spoke to his heart like no one else on Earth. He'd never been in love before—was this what it felt like? Pain and happiness and fear and hope all tangled together? Something you wanted to run away from but couldn't bear to leave?

She walked toward his front door. He raced down the stairs to open it, suddenly freezing in fear with his hand on the knob. *Open the door,* he told himself. *Own up to it and open the door.*

"Can we talk?" she said in a soft, unsteady voice once he opened the door.

"Sure," he said, although it probably sounded more like a mumbled gulp. He pulled the door open and waved her inside.

"You live here?" she asked, looking around at the bland, unremarkable furnishings.

No art hung on the walls, no souvenirs of his world

travels graced the shelves—those things were all in boxes in storage for... For when? It struck him that he didn't know. He'd been in a temporary-transient mode for years. "For now."

"I'm sorry," she said.

Bruce stared at her. Why on earth did she feel *she* needed to apologize to *him*? "Whatever for?"

"I was shocked. And hurt. I never... It just took me so much by surprise. It doesn't seem possible."

He ran one hand over his jaw and realized he must look like how he felt—an utter disaster of a guy. Still, she didn't seem to care. "I should have told you that first day," he admitted. If he'd owned up to it then, they'd never have crossed all those lines that made it hurt so much now. He'd made such a mess of it.

"I know what I said earlier. But, well, I'm glad you didn't." She walked farther into the room, but neither one of them sat down. "All the good things wouldn't have happened if I'd known."

That wasn't a fair trade in his opinion. "You mean, if I hadn't lied to you all that time." It was what he'd done, really. Withholding what he knew—who he was—was as much of a lie as anything, wasn't it?

"You could have never told me at all," she offered.

"No," he replied immediately. "That was never an option. You were going to have to know. I just couldn't... bring myself to tell you. The more I got to know you and the boys, the more I couldn't stand the thought of you hating me."

She did sit down at that statement, perching carefully on the couch with her hands tight in her lap. "It would be easier to hate you. I've resented so much for so long it's all I knew to do. I hated the ocean. I hated the press. I blamed my own decisions. I blamed Rick for insisting the car had to be moved. I blamed God. You start to feel like the anger is the only thing keeping you going, but really it's just eating you up from the inside out."

"I hurt you." It seemed like the only thing to say. "It's tearing me up that I hurt you."

She looked up at him, the sorrow and clarity of those green eyes going right through him. "That's just it, Bruce. You didn't. I'm in pain, yes, but that's not the same thing. I don't think I realized that until last night. We're both in pain." She waved her hand as if reaching for the right words. "We're all hurting. But you didn't hurt me."

"How can you say that? I didn't do what I should have, and you paid the price."

"You didn't know the cost of turning down that assignment. That wasn't some fault of yours any more than my hiding from the water since then. It was just the human response of someone in pain. I never thought I'd be able to say this, but it's not your fault or my fault or Rick's or any of the people who were there when it happened."

Bruce felt all those years of guilt press down on his chest like a vise. He sank down on the sofa next to her. "I don't believe that." He didn't. He wasn't sure he'd ever be able to believe that.

Willa reached out and laid her hand on top of his. "I know. That's why I came here. To tell you that I forgive you of what you think you did to me. You need that. How could I let you drown in all this guilt when I'm the one person who can save you? I forgive you."

Chapter Twenty

It was an astounding thing. Willa felt some hard and bitter shell fall off her soul when the words *I forgive you* left her mouth. This visit was for Bruce, but it turned out it healed her just as much. She'd built Bruce—not even really Bruce, just everything he represented—into an enemy just as fierce as the ocean. But he wasn't. He was just a man, just a soul trying to make it through a world of hurt the same as she was.

But he was also an amazing man. Kind and caring, brave and strong. A man who saw everything in her she was sure she had lost.

"How can you forgive me?" He looked utterly stunned at the notion.

For as large as the question was, the answer came to her with a quick simplicity. "Because you need it. Because I can give it—and I think I need to give it." She reached up and touched his cheek. "And because I care so much about you."

Bruce swallowed hard, his jaw working under her fingers. She saw tears gathering in his eyes. "Willa…"

There was so much in the way he said her name. Wonder and caring and woundedness and hope. A lightness came over her she hadn't known since that splendid kiss last night, and Willa felt a surprising smile turn up the corners of her mouth. "How does it feel to be the one saved instead of the one doing all the saving?"

It was a rather bold thing to say, but the way Bruce's eyes fell shut and the way one tear slid down his broad jaw told her it had been the right thing to do. Her, being the bold one—who would have thought it?

Bruce shook his head. "I don't know how I am going to let such an amazing woman walk out of my life, back to Fort Lauderdale."

"Then don't."

The answer startled her as much as it did Bruce. His eyes opened wide. His jaw gaped for a second before he gulped out, "How?"

"To be honest, I have no idea," she replied, feeling her heart warm at the sense of joyful surprise humming between them. "I think we both thought last night was just one night. What if it isn't?"

"What if it isn't?" he repeated, his eyes aglow. "You and the boys mean so much to me. I know it's impossible, but..."

She laughed. "It's all one giant impossibility, isn't it?" Willa felt light and sparkling at the lifting of all that weight. *Possibility.* When was the last time she'd felt anything close to this sense of possibility?

Bruce stood up and pulled her up as well. "I want to try." He gave her the warmest of smiles. "If you haven't noticed, I seem to have a knack for things that look impossible."

She laughed again. "I had noticed, in fact."

He gazed at her for a long, dizzying moment before touching her cheek with a tenderness that made her reel. "I want you and the boys in my life." With that, he pulled her close and kissed her. The initial, sweet kiss became a powerful one, a declaration of all she knew they both felt. Impossible and yet very, very real. Life-giving. At that moment, it was quite impossible to say who had saved whom. Wasn't that the way love was supposed to be?

She loved him. The wonder of that swept through her as powerfully as Bruce's kiss. She wrapped her arms around his neck and clung to him, feeling saved in every possible way.

He must have noticed the change in her, because Bruce pulled back and looked into her eyes. "I don't mean to shock you, but I am all-out in love with you," he said, looking as if he couldn't help himself. "Can you live with that?"

"You'd be surprised." She kissed him again. "I wondered if I'd ever be in love again. I'm so grateful it's with you."

Bruce picked her up and spun her around, laughing and holding her close. Light seeped into all the dark corners she'd been carrying around for too long. She laughed alongside him, soaking in the sheer joy of the moment.

He set her down but kept his arms around her waist. Willa reveled in how good it felt to rest in his embrace. "How about Jack and Joe? Will they be okay with this?"

"They adore you." They did. "I think they need you in their lives as much as I do."

"We'll figure it out. I'll stop traveling. I'll go work in a hardware store, or a bank, or whatever it takes."

She couldn't picture Bruce in a conventional job. "Oh, I don't think we'll have to go quite that far. Maybe just dial down the danger a bit, and be home more often."

He grinned. "Home. Boy, do I like the sound of that."

She hadn't expected that response. Family life seemed such a far cry from his current nomadic existence. "Really?"

"Really." He sighed deeply. "I'm tired of running, Willa. It's not the same thing as adventure, even when you tell yourself it is."

She raised an eyebrow at his dramatic statement. "An ordinary life with two grade school boys might strike you as kind of boring."

He dismissed that with a grin and a quick kiss. "Not a chance." How completely, utterly changed he was from the man who'd opened his door a short while ago. For that matter, so was she. "Not with you. You are anything but ordinary."

Willa felt as if she were glowing. "I've felt so…broken…for so long. Just one big pile of 'not enough.' Not strong enough, not wise enough, not healed enough—take your pick. But when you showed me that photo, I saw a different woman. You could have told me she was there, and I wouldn't have believed you. But she was there. Do you have any idea what that did to me? For me?"

He touched her cheek again, erasing any doubt that daring to come here was the right thing to do. *Thank You for not allowing me to let this slip away.*

"I knew then, by the way. The moment I took that photo, I knew I'd fallen for you." He smiled. "I had no idea what to do about it, and it scared me to death—but like you said, photographs never lie."

"Where is he, Mom? Why isn't Mr. Bruce here? He needs to know the ducklings hatched this morning. Is he not coming back?" The boys had been pestering her with questions since breakfast. Fortunately, Jack and Joe were too busy having fun in the kitchen to miss her until she returned to camp with Seb's Jeep. Still, breakfast had been a challenge. Even Seb's wonderful pancakes—which the boys had insisted they'd played a big part in making—were hard to eat. After all, she had just declared her heart to the last man she'd ever have guessed. The world had upended itself and yet somehow righted itself at the same time. Nothing was the same; nothing in her future was any more set than when she got off that bus weeks ago—but things were better. Far better than she ever could have imagined.

"He'll be here," she said, helping Joe make his bed. "I promise he'll be here."

Jack slumped down on his bunk. "I don't wanna go back to Florida," he whined. "I like it here. Can we live here?"

Willa had to admit, leaving here did pull on her heart. In the space of three weeks, Camp True North Springs had become dear to her. And to think how she'd dreaded coming here, how she'd been so uncomfortable those first few days.

She smoothed the boys' hair. "I know it's hard. We've had lots of fun here. But we still have one more day."

"It's not enough. I really like the food," Jack offered. "We made great pancakes. And Chef Seb makes good tacos."

"The food is good." Willa tucked the laundry they'd done in preparation for packing into a drawer. They were taking home so much more than dusty clothes from their time here. She still couldn't believe they would be finding a way to add Bruce into their lives, too.

She hadn't told the twins yet—Bruce had asked to be the one to tell them. *He cares so much for Jack and Joe. What a gift that is.* "There's going to be a big reunion party here in the fall, you know. I've already told Mr. Mason and Ms. Dana that we will come back for that."

"Yay!" The boys cheered the news with happy shouts. "We get to come back!"

As she pulled Jack's camera from its charger and handed it to him—the device practically never left his side since Bruce had given it to him—Willa heard the sound of tires on the parking lot gravel.

Joe, who could see the parking lot from where he was sitting, perked up immediately. "It's Mr. Bruce! He's here!"

Willa's heart glowed at the thought of seeing Bruce again. He'd let her head on back to camp, confessing he needed badly to clean up. But not before one last breathtaking kiss. He'd promised to be in Florida by the end of the month, but she was already dreading his absence as much as the boys were dreading leaving camp. How much had changed in the last few hours.

Joe waved wildly as Jack joined him at the open window. "Hi, Mr. Bruce! You missed it—the ducklings hatched!"

Bruce's smile upon seeing the boys sank deep into Willa with a warm assurance. "That's great news!" he called out. "Can I come in and see you?"

"Sure," Joe replied.

Bruce raised an eyebrow. "Don't you think you should ask your mom?"

"Nah," Jack said with startling confidence. Knowing what was coming, Willa could only smile. In fact, she hadn't stopped smiling since she returned from Bruce's rental, and more than one person had noticed.

The twins dashed over to the door, flinging it open before Bruce had even made it down the hall. The sweet sight of them tumbling onto him and pulling him into the room only confirmed what Willa already knew— they were bonded together with more than enough care to conquer any of the pain.

After an assortment of both silly and practical questions about ducklings and everything else, Bruce sat the boys down on the lower bunk and pulled up the chair from the room's small desk to face them. "Listen, boys, I've got something serious to talk to you about."

Their exuberance dissolved into a pair of anxious faces. "Okay."

Willa sat leaning against the desk, charmed by the importance Bruce gave the conversation. He actually looked nervous. She couldn't imagine the boys giving any resistance to what he would say, but it touched her how much he cared to take their feelings into account.

"It's about your mom," Bruce began.

This took Joe by surprise. "What about Mom?"

Bruce looked down for a moment, steepling his hands with his elbows on his knees. He was reaching for the right words, and even she was wondering how he would explain things.

"Well, the thing is, I really like your mom."

Jack didn't quite seem to see why this needed to be such a serious subject. "Lots of people like Mom."

"Well," said Bruce, looking a bit flustered. "I happen to like your mom *a whole lot*. More than anybody else here, I expect—except for you two, of course."

Joe thought about this for a moment, eyebrows furrowed. "Is that bad?"

Bruce chuckled while Willa tried to muffle her own laugh. "No," he answered. "It's good. Really good."

Jack looked from Bruce to his mother. "Does she like you back? A whole lot?"

Despite her cheeks turning what had to be bright pink, Willa replied, "Yes, I do. A whole lot."

Bruce caught her gaze for a sparkling second before returning his attention to the boys. "So I was hoping maybe we could be friends even after camp is over. See a lot of each other. Spend time together."

"But you live here," Joe said.

"Well, actually, I don't live much of anywhere. And I'm tired of that. So…" Bruce ran his hands over his knees. She'd never seen him so charmingly unnerved. "I was thinking maybe I might come live in Florida where you are."

Jack didn't need even a second to mull that over. "Really? That's great! You could come help me take more pictures and stuff."

"Yep." Bruce looked at Joe. "That okay with you?"

"I think so," Joe said, "But why is Mom crying? Does Mom not want you to come?"

Willa hadn't even realized the tears were on her cheeks. Bruce reached back and took her hand, and it was the easiest thing in the world to let her fingers intertwine with his. "Oh yes," she answered her son. "I want Mr. Bruce to come to Florida. I want to spend lots of time with him."

"So you're happy, not sad." Joe was trying to work it out—especially the part about how his mother was now holding hands with Mr. Bruce.

"Very happy," Willa said, feeling Bruce give her fingers a squeeze. "And I'm glad you're happy about it, too."

"Me too," Bruce said, giving her a radiant look. "I'm super happy about it."

"Are you coming home with us tomorrow? On the plane?" Jack asked.

"No, not yet. There are a few things I need to do here. But it'll be soon, I promise." Bruce squeezed her hands again. "Hey, I heard you guys made pancakes."

"We did! We're really good at it, too," Joe boasted.

"Do you think you could duck over to the kitchen and ask Chef Seb if he has any left?"

"Sure." With that, the pair scrambled to the door and dashed across the bit of ground between the barn guest rooms and the big house.

The second Jack and Joe were out of sight, Bruce pulled Willa to him and kissed her again. It took her breath away, just like the others.

"That's going to take some getting used to," she mused, enjoying how light and carefree she felt that morning.

Bruce kept her close. "Do you think they figured it out?"

She laughed. "They're six. They don't even understand cooties yet, much less girls." She looked up to meet Bruce's eyes. "It's all pretty much beyond understanding, don't you think?"

"Mason would call this a God thing. He said so when I first saw you, when I barreled into his office and told him I had to leave immediately."

"I'm so glad you didn't." She sighed. "It is a God thing, isn't it? There's no other explanation."

"No other needed," Bruce replied. He took her hand and pulled her toward the door. "Come on. I missed breakfast. And I think there are a few people we need to let in on a big secret."

Together, Willa and Bruce walked toward the big house—and toward the extraordinary future God had prepared for them.

Epilogue

Fall

Bruce stood with Mason under an enormous sign that read "Camp True North Springs Family Reunion." The camp director clasped Bruce's shoulder with a wide smile on his face. "This is so much better than I imagined."

"It is pretty amazing," Bruce agreed. His friend looked thrilled. Dana was bursting with pride, and the big-house dining room was filled to capacity. Bruce had always known the release of the photo book and tonight's reunion fundraiser would be a smashing success, but he had to agree with Mason that things had exceeded expectations.

And Mason didn't even know the additional surprise Bruce had planned.

Seb walked up to Willa and the boys. "What are you feeding these two? They're growing like weeds."

"We're in first grade now," Jack boasted.

"And looking good," Seb replied. "I'm glad to see you. Did you say hello to Charlie? Champion and Marshall are here, too." The chef shook Bruce's hand.

"Florida agrees with you. Or is it just a certain Florida family?"

Bruce didn't bother to tamp down his grin. "I think you know the answer to that." He looked around the bustling room. He'd taken and organized so many portraits that he felt like he knew each family in the room. Seb's wife, Kate, with their two children, Kimmy and Kent, were over at one table, talking with a woman Bruce recognized as Martina Garza and her son, Matteo. You'd never know from looking at the little guy that he'd battled cancer and a stem cell transplant. In fact, the room was packed with stories of triumph over tragedy. It had been one of the greatest honors of his life to document those stories for the books now stacked at the far end of the room.

Bridget Todd, the camp nurse, waddled slowly over to Willa with one hand on her back. "I don't know how you did it," she moaned. "Being pregnant with twins is tough."

Bruce shook Carson Todd's hand. "Congratulations. Twin girls, huh? Your life is about to get really interesting."

Carson laughed. "My life's about to get very sleep deprived. I might need to stay away from the power tools until preschool."

"We'll be taking next summer's session off," Bridget announced. "For obvious reasons."

"May I have your attention for a moment," Dana announced from beside the table of books. "I know you all want to talk with each other, but we just want to say a few words to mark the occasion."

Charlie stepped up next to her holding a card. "I get

the best job. I get to announce that we've raised sixty thousand dollars to support all the stuff here at camp."

Cheers and applause filled the room.

Willa leaned in to Bruce. "That's way over the goal, isn't it?"

Bruce smiled. "Wasn't hard once word got out about all the good things that happen here."

Mason stepped up next. "We're so thankful. God has provided so much for us. And we're so happy all of you have returned to celebrate. We want these books to serve as a remembrance for each of you. So there's a book for everyone and a bunch of pens. Please take a book and have everyone sign their photograph, like a yearbook. Share your memories with each other. We plan to do a book like this every year, and keep one copy in the house library with all your signatures."

"That's a wonderful idea," Willa said. "Did you come up with that?"

"No, that was Mason's idea," Bruce replied. "But the next part is all mine."

"I want our photographer to come up and take a bow," Mason said. "And maybe say a few words."

Bruce kept Willa's hand in his as he walked toward the front of the room, letting go only when he reached the table. He'd thought this through a hundred times—it had to be perfect.

He cleared his throat and addressed the crowd. "It's been a privilege to gather your photos and take so many of your portraits. I know I tend to exaggerate, but it's no exaggeration to say this book and this camp changed my life. I've never been more proud of a project." He reached for a book at the back of the stacks, sending an oversize wink to Jack as he did so. Jack nodded and pulled up his camera, ready to take the shot they'd arranged in secret. "So if you'll indulge me, I'd like Willa to be the first one to sign my book."

Willa blushed, but Joe was right beside her, nudging her up to where Bruce was standing. Bruce handed her the book, trying hard to ensure his hands didn't shake when he did so. "Page fourteen," he cued. He reached into his pocket while she flipped the book open to the page, then held his breath until she read what he'd written there.

She gasped, gave a small cry and looked up at him.

He was vaguely aware of the other people in the room, slightly registering the sound of Jack snapping photographs. Everything else was all about how Willa looked, the shock and delight in those stunning green eyes, and the tears that brimmed there. For a moment, no one spoke.

At least until Joe yelled out, "What's it say, Mom?" He may or may not have been coached to do something of that sort.

Bruce nodded while Willa tried to find her voice. "It says, 'Will you marry me?'"

An even bigger set of cheers filled the room as Bruce got down on one knee, holding out the ring. Willa was clutching the book, taking deep breaths and generally trying not to sob. "Yes," she finally managed, sending the crowd into wild applause.

He slipped the ring onto her finger just before Jack and Joe crashed into the two of them, a tiny twin tornado of happy shouts. "We all say yes!" Joe announced.

"Well, I suppose you *are* marrying all of us," Willa

said, half laughing and half crying. It felt as if all the world's happiness had poured itself into this one room.

"I wouldn't have it any other way." With that, Bruce kissed the woman who would be his wife. He'd found his home in Willa, and that was worth everything.

Rita Salinas, whom Bruce had learned was one of the camp's staunchest supporters from the very beginning, clasped her hands. "Camp True North Springs has quite a talent for matchmaking, don't you think? Dana and Mason, Seb and Kate, Bridget and Carson, and now you two."

Bruce could only grin at Mason and Dana, whose match had started it all. "I get the feeling we won't be the last."

"Maybe we should call it Camp True Love Springs," Rita's husband, Bart, said with a laugh.

"No way," Charlie declared. "That's mushy."

While mushy definitely had its virtues, Bruce had to agree. "I think it's perfect just the way it is." And with that, he gave his future wife a very mushy, very wonderful kiss.

* * * * *

Dear Reader,

I hope you have enjoyed these visits to Camp True North Springs as much as I have. The big house, barn guest rooms, memorial garden and pond have become near and dear to me as they welcome the families who visit. And the staff feel like fond friends I want to keep in my life for a long time.

Bruce and Willa each have enormous challenges on their way to their different kinds of healing. While it seems like a cruel twist at first, their mutual arrival at camp is merely God's hand working to meet their deepest need. I love how twins Jack and Joe also draw them forward in the way that only children seem able to do. I pray this story gives you hope that Our Lord will indeed meet your needs—even if in wildly unexpected and challenging ways.

If you've not read the three other books in the series, I invite you to go back and discover the other stories: *A Place to Heal*, *Restoring Their Family* and *The Nurse's Homecoming*.

As always, I love to hear from readers. You can find me on Instagram, Facebook, Twitter, or email me at allie@alliepleiter.com.

Take care, and be on the lookout for fresh new adventures from me in the future!

Blessings,
Allie

COMING NEXT MONTH FROM
Love Inspired

THE WIDOW'S BACHELOR BARGAIN
Brides of Lost Creek • by Marta Perry

When her sons discover a teenage girl sleeping in the barn, Amish widow Dorcas Bitler finds herself caught between the rebellious runaway and Jacob Unger, the girl's stubborn uncle. Dorcas is determined to mend their relationship...but falling for Jacob was never part of the plan.

THEIR FORBIDDEN AMISH MATCH
by Lucy Bayer

Hoping to meet the brother he's never known, doctor Todd Barrett arrives in Hickory Hollow, Ohio, full of hope—but immediately clashes with local Amish midwife Lena Hochstetler. They don't seem to agree on anything...until they discover deeper feelings that just might complicate both their lives.

THEIR INSEPARABLE BOND
K-9 Companions • by Jill Weatherholt

Olivia Hart has one goal: to convince her ailing grandmother to move to Florida with her. The last thing she expects is for service dog trainer and single dad Jake Beckett to change *her* mind. Will a rambunctious puppy and twins bring two reluctant hearts together?

A VALENTINE'S DAY RETURN
Sunset Ridge • by Brenda Minton

Ending his marriage to his childhood sweetheart was the biggest mistake Mark Rivers ever made. But now he's back to make amends with Kylie and their daughter. When a health crisis draws them closer, will Mark prove he's the man his family needs...or has he lost them both for good?

A BABY IN ALASKA
Home to Hearts Bay • by Heidi McCahan

After arriving in Alaska for a wedding and business trip—with his newly orphaned baby nephew in tow—Sam Frazier knows he's in over his head. He has no choice but to accept help from feisty pilot Rylee Madden. Their arrangement is temporary, but caring for baby Silas might make their love permanent...

HER CHANCE AT FAMILY
by Angie Dicken

As the guardian of her orphaned nieces, interior designer Elisa Hartley is too busy to think about being jilted on her wedding day. *Almost.* Besides, she's already growing feelings for her new landscape architect, Sean Peters...until she discovers the secret he's been hiding.

LICNM1223

Get 3 FREE REWARDS!

We'll send you 2 FREE Books plus a FREE Mystery Gift.

FREE Value Over **$20**

Both the **Love Inspired**® and **Love Inspired**® **Suspense** series feature compelling novels filled with inspirational romance, faith, forgiveness and hope.

YES! Please send me 2 FREE novels from the Love Inspired or Love Inspired Suspense series and my FREE gift (gift is worth about $10 retail). After receiving them, if I don't wish to receive any more books, I can return the shipping statement marked "cancel." If I don't cancel, I will receive 6 brand-new Love Inspired Larger-Print books or Love Inspired Suspense Larger-Print books every month and be billed just $6.49 each in the U.S. or $6.74 each in Canada. That is a savings of at least 16% off the cover price. It's quite a bargain! Shipping and handling is just 50¢ per book in the U.S. and $1.25 per book in Canada.* I understand that accepting the 2 free books and gift places me under no obligation to buy anything. I can always return a shipment and cancel at any time by calling the number below. The free books and gift are mine to keep no matter what I decide.

Choose one: ☐ **Love Inspired Larger-Print** (122/322 BPA GRPA) ☐ **Love Inspired Suspense Larger-Print** (107/307 BPA GRPA) ☐ **Or Try Both!** (122/322 & 107/307 BPA GRRP)

Name (please print)

Address _____ Apt. #

City _____ State/Province _____ Zip/Postal Code

Email: Please check this box ☐ if you would like to receive newsletters and promotional emails from Harlequin Enterprises ULC and its affiliates. You can unsubscribe anytime.

> Mail to the **Harlequin Reader Service:**
> **IN U.S.A.:** P.O. Box 1341, Buffalo, NY 14240-8531
> **IN CANADA:** P.O. Box 603, Fort Erie, Ontario L2A 5X3

Want to try 2 free books from another series! Call 1-800-873-8635 or visit www.ReaderService.com.

*Terms and prices subject to change without notice. Prices do not include sales taxes, which will be charged (if applicable) based on your state or country of residence. Canadian residents will be charged applicable taxes. Offer not valid in Quebec. This offer is limited to one order per household. Books received may not be as shown. Not valid for current subscribers to the Love Inspired or Love Inspired Suspense series. All orders subject to approval. Credit or debit balances in a customer's account(s) may be offset by any other outstanding balance owed by or to the customer. Please allow 4 to 6 weeks for delivery. Offer available while quantities last.

Your Privacy—Your information is being collected by Harlequin Enterprises ULC, operating as Harlequin Reader Service. For a complete summary of the information we collect, how we use this information and to whom it is disclosed, please visit our privacy notice located at corporate.harlequin.com/privacy-notice. From time to time we may also exchange your personal information with reputable third parties. If you wish to opt out of this sharing of your personal information, please visit readerservice.com/consumerschoice or call 1-800-873-8635. **Notice to California Residents**—Under California law, you have specific rights to control and access your data. For more information on these rights and how to exercise them, visit corporate.harlequin.com/california-privacy.

LIRLIS23